MISSION: HER SAFETY

TEAM 52 #5

ANNA HACKETT

Mission: Her Safety

Published by Anna Hackett

Copyright 2019 by Anna Hackett

Cover by Melody Simmons of BookCoversCre8tive

Cover Image by FuriousFotog / Golden Czermak

Edits by Tanya Saari

ISBN (ebook): 978-1-925539-72-1

ISBN (paperback): 978-1-925539-73-8

Unexplored – Romantic Book of the Year (Ruby) Novella Winner 2017

Unfathomed and Unmapped - Romantic Book of the Year (Ruby) finalists 2018

At Star's End – One of Library Journal's Best E-Original Romances for 2014

Return to Dark Earth – One of Library Journal's Best E-Original Books for 2015 and two-time SFR Galaxy Awards winner

The Phoenix Adventures – SFR Galaxy Award Winner for Most Fun New Series and "Why Isn't This a Movie?" Series

Beneath a Trojan Moon – SFR Galaxy Award Winner and RWAus Ella Award Winner

Hell Squad – SFR Galaxy Award for best Post-Apocalypse for Readers who don't like Post-Apocalypse

The Anomaly Series – #1 Amazon Action Adventure Romance Bestseller

"Like Indiana Jones meets Star Wars. A treasure hunt with a steamy romance." – SFF Dragon, review of *Among Galactic Ruins*

"Strap in, enjoy the heat of romance and the daring of this group of space travellers!" – Di, Top 500 Amazon Reviewer, review of *At Star's End*

"Action, danger, aliens, romance – yup, it's another great book from Anna Hackett!" – Book Gannet Reviews, review of *Hell Squad: Marcus*

Sign up for my VIP mailing list and get your *free box set* containing three action-packed romances.

Visit here to get started:
www.annahackettbooks.com

CHAPTER ONE

W ith the flashlight clamped in her teeth, she finished unfastening the screws and carefully nudged the panel aside.

Shifting carefully in the cramped ventilation duct, River Elliott-Hall pulled her small snake camera from her pocket. She lowered the flexible cord down through the hole she'd just opened up, and pulled her phone out. The screen blinked to life, showing a full view of the room below.

All clear.

Smiling, she tucked the camera and her phone into the pockets at the sides of her tight, black leggings. She gripped the edge of the hole and then tipped forward, rolling slowly down. She let go, landed in a crouch, then rose.

Thanks for the training, MI6.

Thinking of her old job made her belly hard. She

shut those thoughts down instantly, and focused on scanning the long room that housed the art gallery.

Her gaze skated over all the priceless paintings on the walls and sculptures resting on ornate pedestals. The wealthy owner of the Constellation Casino in Las Vegas had spared no expense for the private art gallery on the top floor of his casino. In addition to the artwork, there was a lot of imported Italian marble and gold-plated trim.

Despite Chadwick Alton's massive bank balance, the man had no taste. Her lip curled. She also knew he was one step below scum of the Earth for a variety of reasons.

Focus, River. Stomach tight, she tucked back a curl that had escaped from her hair tie. She kept her mass of tight curls pulled back securely when she was working. It didn't pay to have your hair in the way when you were breaking and entering.

She pulled a small, metallic ball from her pocket and then rolled it across the marble floor. It slowed, then broke apart with a click. Blue light shone out of it, illuminating several red laser beams that crisscrossed the hall, part of the gallery's high-tech security system.

The ball beeped. The lasers flickered off.

River smiled. No fancy laser dancing for her. She preferred using the tech she paid a small fortune for to make her job a little easier.

She moved silently down the gallery, shining the light on the paintings. She had a job to do, and she prided herself on her one-hundred-percent success rate.

The gallery was a long rectangle, and on one side, curved windows gave a view of both Las Vegas' blinking lights and the vast desert beyond. Being a new casino, the

Constellation wasn't right in the heart of the Strip, but rather, to the northern end.

On the other wall, she spied several well-known and expensive paintings on the wall.

But none of them were the stolen masterpiece she was looking for.

At the end of the room, she stopped in front of the pride of the collection. A dramatic Rubens that she knew was worth just over a hundred million dollars.

River carefully lifted the large frame off the wall and gently set it down. Behind it, sat a sleek, metallic, vault door embedded in the wall.

She pulled her streamlined backpack off and pulled out gear. She pried off the keypad covering the electronic lock and plugged in her sweet little codebreaking device.

With a touch of a button, she set her code-breaking program running. She'd hired a reclusive Russian scientist with an off-the-charts IQ to create it for her.

She watched the numbers tick by on her screen.

Beep.

The vault opened.

River looked at her chunky Rolex. She had two minutes until the guard did his rounds.

She pulled the door open and stepped into the vault.

More paintings were stacked against the wall, and the shelves at the back of the vault were packed with boxes that she knew contained jewelry and other precious artifacts.

River quickly looked through the paintings.

Then she cursed, her stomach curdling. The painting wasn't here.

She'd been hired to do a job, an important one. *Bloody hell.* She looked at her watch again. Time was almost up.

She exited the vault and closed it. Using extreme care, she set the multi-million-dollar Rubens back in place. Then she turned and jogged down the gallery. At the end, she jumped up, and grabbed the edge of the hole. She pulled herself back up and then set the panel back in place.

She paused, and a moment later, she heard the footsteps of the guard.

River smiled. Then, she turned and started crawling through the vent.

After a few tight squeezes, she dropped down through a panel that she'd loosened earlier and into a maintenance closet. She found the bag she'd stashed behind some mops. She slid her smaller backpack inside, then quickly wrapped a red scarf around her neck and pulled on a beaten leather jacket.

Then she pulled the hair tie out of her hair, letting her curls spring free. The tight coils bounced around just above her shoulders.

She slid out of the door of the maintenance closet and closed it behind her. She sauntered down the empty corridor and then heard the click of heels. A casino cocktail waitress, wearing a tiny slip of sparkly black and some feathers, passed her, carrying a tray. The woman gave River a tired nod.

A second later, River stepped out into the casino. As she sauntered across the main floor, the rush of noise and color hit her—the tinkle of slot machine tunes, laughter, the clack of a roulette wheel.

She moved like she had all the time in the world. Her MI6 partner, Jack, had taught her that the best way to sneak in where you didn't belong was to always look like you *did* belong. *Don't rush, River. Own it.* Her throat tightened.

A man sitting at a blackjack table lifted his head and his gaze caught hers. Appreciation flared, his gaze drifting down her long body.

River shot him a wide smile and a wink. Then she was clear of the tables and moving across the vast Constellation lobby.

Finally, she stepped outside, shaking her head at the approaching valet. She jogged down the front steps and out on the Las Vegas Boulevard. Two minutes later, she moved down a side street and into the lot where she'd left her rental car.

With a bleep of the locks, she slid inside the sleek, sporty Mercedes. The engine vibrated to life, and River zipped out of the parking lot. She joined the traffic on the Strip, and glanced in her rearview mirror. Her gaze stayed on the shiny, black façade of the Constellation, with all the twinkling lights that lit up the side, just like a constellation of stars.

She blew out a breath. Dammit, that had been her best lead. And deep in her bones, she'd wanted it to be Alton. Wanted to expose the charlatan under the expensive suit.

Don't. Get. Personal.

Another of Jack's lessons. She followed the street

signs and got onto the highway heading east. As she moved onto the four-lane highway, she sped up, gunning the Mercedes' engine. Back in London, she didn't bother owning a car, so she liked to get the most out of her rentals.

Zipping around several cars, she drummed her fingers on the steering wheel, working out her next steps.

All she could do was follow up on her less-promising lead.

Team 52.

River had heard a lot of rumors about the team. She'd read some classified documents on them back at MI6. Black ops. Highly classified. From what she'd pieced together, their job was to safeguard powerful historical artifacts.

She'd been shocked as hell to discover that civilization had been a lot more advanced than most people, and the history books, believed. Humans had done amazing things before the flooding at the end of the last ice age had ruined it all and acted like a reset button. But a few things had survived.

Now, if something got uncovered that had unexplained abilities, Team 52 swooped in.

No doubt the American government had a nice little vault somewhere filled with fascinating, interesting things for them to test and experiment with. She had no doubt the British government had one too.

It sounded crazy, but she'd seen some inexplicable things as an agent. Hell, she saw some mind-blowing things now that she was freelance, as well.

Jack would have laughed at it all.

Jack. Her hands clenched on the wheel. Her mentor, the man who'd taught her everything, was gone. Long gone.

River pressed her foot down on the accelerator.

Soon, she left the lights of Las Vegas behind. Ahead, stark mountains rose up, nothing like England's green, rolling hills. She turned off the highway and ended up on a narrow dirt road. She stopped at a gate, looking beyond it at the rustic cabin in the distance.

She knew that two Team 52 members called this little cabin home. From her recon, she also knew they were currently away from home and busy with work.

After turning her car around, she climbed out and quickly climbed over the fence. She'd barely taken two steps when her phone beeped. With a low curse, she pulled her high-tech phone out. Dammit, it looked like Smith Creed had a fancy detection system set up around his cabin.

River swiped the screen of her phone and pulled up an app. She touched a button and jammed the security system.

Then she walked toward the front door of the cabin.

"Woof."

She froze and watched a huge, blue-gray Great Dane lope around the side of the cabin.

Fuck.

"Hey, sweetie," River said.

The dog growled at her.

Hmm. Luckily, she was always prepared for any situation. She opened a small pouch on her belt and pulled out some jerky. She tossed it at the dog.

He bristled, but when she didn't move, he sniffed the jerky suspiciously. Then he licked it and gave her what she could only describe as a dirty look.

River stiffened, but then the dog wolfed the jerky down in a couple of gulps.

She tried not to tap her boot as she waited. She wondered briefly if there was enough sedative in the jerky for such a big dog.

The Great Dane kept his gaze locked on her and she boldly returned it. *I'm the alpha here, buddy.*

A second later, the dog took a wobbly step forward. He let out a whine, then dropped to the ground. She forced herself to wait and make sure he was out.

River moved over and checked him. He was breathing fine and she released a breath, then allowed herself a few strokes of his fur. She traveled too much to have a pet, but she'd always wanted one.

"Sorry, big guy."

Then she snapped on some gloves and pulled out her lockpicks. It took a little while to get through the locks on the cabin door. Muttering a curse, she made a mental note to remember that Creed did not muck around with his security.

The door swung open and she stepped inside. She liked it. It was rustic, with lots of stone and wood, but touches of cute. There were some perky, yellow flowers on the kitchen counter, and candles lined the shelves.

She quickly moved through the space, searching for anything relevant to her hunt for the stolen painting.

She saw a framed photo sitting on the mantel. She studied the picture of the huge man—Creed was a former

Navy SEAL—and the smaller, gorgeous blonde beside him. The woman had a movie-star smile, and she was looking up at the man beside her like he was her reason for breathing. And the way Creed kept her tucked in tight under his arm stated his claim.

They were clearly in love. River shook her head. She gave them a year. Love was one of life's biggest cons.

She made short work of searching the rest of the cabin. There was nothing about their work. Nothing about the *Salvator Mundi*.

Bugger. River shoved her hands on her hips. She'd known it was a long shot—none of the other Team 52 residences she'd searched had yielded anything either.

Carefully, she walked out and locked the door. As she skirted the sleeping dog, her boots kicking up dust, she ran through her options.

She was too cautious not to finish searching the rest of the team's places. There was a small chance that the team had taken the *Salvator Mundi*. The trail she'd managed to follow from the museum that owned the painting led to Las Vegas. And Las Vegas was the home base for Team 52.

She'd already checked the condo belonging to the team's leader, Lachlan Hunter. His security system had been top-notch and she'd been forced to fork out extra money for some more gear to crack it. After that, she'd searched the house where the team's second-in-command, Blair Mason, lived with her police detective lover. And River had also checked the converted warehouse belonging to the team's scientist.

The man had almost caught her. River sniffed. It had

been a little too close for comfort. Especially since he blew all nerdy scientist stereotypes out of the water. Dr. Ty Sampson was big, muscled, and in top shape.

Shaking off her near miss, she focused on the places she still had to check—former Delta Force operator, Axel Diaz, the team medic, Callie Kimura, the team tech guy, Brooks Jameson, and former CIA-agent, Seth Lynch.

Whatever it took, she would find the *Salvator Mundi*. Finding people and things was what she did, and she was the best. She *never* failed.

Well, she had once, and her partner had paid the price.

Jaw tight, River headed back to her rental. Failure wasn't an option. Never, ever again.

DR. TY SAMPSON lifted his goggles onto the top of his head.

He stared at the small, wooden box resting on the bench in his lab. It had just clicked open.

Incredible.

After several hours of careful work, he'd managed to open the old box that had come from a dig in India. And inside, was a large, blue gemstone. This had been hidden from human eyes for hundreds of years.

He narrowed his gaze. He guessed the stone was about seventy carats, and likely a blue diamond—but he'd have to run several tests to confirm it.

And also to see what else it could do.

That was his main role at Area 52. He helped study

the artifacts that the team brought in. Some, so he could neutralize them and ensure they stayed safely locked away. Others, to research their powerful abilities and determine if there were ways to utilize them.

Advanced cultures had once possessed ancient technology that was mind-boggling. It was just unfortunate that so much of it had been destroyed, leaving humans to develop so much all over again.

Although, seeing what the assholes who got their hands on the pieces of old tech wanted to do with it—generally to promote their own foul agendas and line their pockets—it might be best if most of the artifacts stayed locked away in the Area 52 warehouse.

When any of the artifacts proved too dangerous, they went straight in the warehouse, under lock and key.

Ty straightened, tension running along his back and shoulders. He moved his neck and heard it crack, then he blew out a breath. Usually, being in his lab and absorbed in his work soothed him.

Not today.

He was still thinking of the intruder he'd had at his place the other night.

Who was she? What the hell was she doing in his warehouse?

After he'd chased her off, he'd searched his renovated warehouse—both the half he'd converted into an apartment and the half that housed his home lab. Nothing had been missing. And she'd left nothing behind.

Ty scowled. He *hated* people in his space. He *hated* people in his lab.

And more than anything, he hated a mystery he couldn't solve.

Ever since he was eight, and had made his own lab in the corner of his parents' giant, eight-car garage, he'd loved working, loved solving problems. For Ty, there was nothing better than pulling things apart to see how they worked, then putting them back together and making them better.

His lab had horrified his parents. They'd returned from their summer vacation in the south of France, and looked aghast at the mess he'd made. But Ty had fought for it, and they'd finally allowed him to keep that little space.

He thought of his mystery woman again. He wanted to solve this mystery. Who the hell was she?

His gaze ran down the long benches in his lab—a far cry from that crowded, cobbled-together space in his parents' garage. His lab at Area 52 was top of the line.

Next to the ancient box he'd just opened was a large ceramic jar. It had been confiscated from a terrorist cell in Iraq. It was old and they'd likely dug it up from some ancient ruin in the desert. Scans showed something particularly volatile inside, but Ty was still trying to ascertain the safest way to open it.

At the far end of the bench, a prototype prosthetic arm rested on two metallic clamps.

All of the members of Team 52 were former military, and many of them had suffered terrible injuries that had ended their careers...until Director Grayson, the man in charge of Area 52, had given them a second chance. And Ty had given them all high-tech prosthetics.

He shoved his hands in the pockets of his lab coat. He should be working on that new prototype he planned to use on the team's leader, Lachlan Hunter. Or on some of the other protype gadgets he had in the works.

That was his second role at Team 52. He put his penchant for inventing to good use. Jonah Grayson gave him a near-unlimited budget. All the team's high-tech gadgets and vehicles were Ty's designs.

He had a lot to do, but today he was just too amped up to get anything useful done.

The lab door opened, and he heard the click of heels on the tile floor. He lifted his head and watched Dr. Natalie Blackwell, Team 52's archeologist, enter.

"Hi, Ty." She tossed her long, black hair over her shoulder. It was in loose waves today. As usual, she was dressed in a tight, gray skirt that hit below her knees, topped with a crisp, pale-pink shirt.

He grunted.

Nat rolled her eyes. "Nice to see you, too." Her soft, Australian accent did nothing to hide her sarcasm. She was gorgeous, smart, and Ty enjoyed working with her.

He grunted again.

"I see you're in an extra cheery mood today."

"I'm working."

Ignoring him, she wandered closer, her gaze falling on the box and blue jewel. She gasped. "You got the box open!"

"Yeah."

She walked past the stone jar, and suddenly, it moved. Ty straightened.

The lid rose up all by itself.

13

He frowned. "What the—?"

Flames flashed out of the vase.

Ty dove on Nat. She cried out and he knocked her to the ground, covering her body with his. He felt a flash of heat on his back.

She gave a short scream, then Ty was up, dragging her away from the flames.

Once they reached the far wall, they both turned, staring in horror at the flames licking the lab bench.

Ty lunged for the high-tech extinguisher he'd designed himself attached to the wall. He lifted the nozzle and started spraying the flames. At the same moment, the experimental fire suppression system he'd designed for the lab came on. It sprayed a gentle mist of suppressant in the exact area of the fire.

It was the first thing Ty had worked on when he'd been recruited from DARPA—the Defense Advanced Research Projects Agency—to join Team 52. The last thing he needed was his inventions, lab equipment, and the priceless artifacts being doused in water that could damage them.

The flames died and Ty straightened. *Fuck.* He set the extinguisher aside.

"Well, I guess we know what that jar does, now." Nat pushed her tangled hair out of her face and pulled on the hem of her shirt. Nothing ruffled Nat for long.

But he heard the tremor in her voice. He tipped her chin up and looked into her dark eyes, checking she wasn't injured.

"Okay?" he asked.

She nodded and rose to her full height. "Thanks for

the rescue, Ty. I'm surprised you jumped on me and not one of your prototypes."

He tapped her nose. "I can rebuild prototypes."

She smiled. "I think I'm going to get a drink." She sighed. "I wish Jonah would allow alcohol on the base."

"You'll survive."

She poked her tongue out at him and headed out.

Ty picked up the phone and made a call to maintenance. He needed them in here to fix the bench and fire damage, and take away the ruined gear.

It wasn't long before three men in black uniforms and tool belts appeared.

"Fix the fire damage, but don't touch anything else," he ordered.

"Yes, sir."

Ty crossed his arms over his chest and as one young man got too close to Ty's equipment, he scowled. The man grew more and more nervous under Ty's stare.

One of the other men cleared his throat. "It might go quicker if you left us to it."

Ty released a breath. "Fine, but remember—"

"Don't touch anything else. We know."

Spinning on his heel, Ty headed for the computer room. If he couldn't work in his lab, then he'd go and harass the team's computer guru about what he'd discovered about Ty's intruder.

Because more than anything, he wanted to know who the hell she was, and why she'd been in his place.

The door to the comp room whispered open, and the man standing at the large, central table raised his head.

Brooks was a computer geek, but he also had a muscled body and ink running down his arms.

Today, the former Navy Intelligence officer wore a T-shirt that stretched over his chest with "Support the troops" written on it, and a picture of a stormtrooper helmet. Ty shook his head.

Brooks smiled. "Hey, Big T."

"I've told you not to call me that."

Brooks grinned at his tablet, before turning to look at the screens covering the walls.

That's when Ty noticed the camera footage that was playing. Team 52, all in their black body armor, were standing in the empty fuselage of a large cargo plane.

"Three, two, one go!" Lachlan yelled.

The team all leaped out of the open Hercules one at a time.

"Training session," Brooks said. "HALO dive."

Ty watched the feed from Lachlan's helmet cam, as the team moved in formation in the air. They were all talking calmly through their earpieces, even though they were jumping out of a perfectly good plane.

"Any updates on the woman who broke into my place?" Ty asked.

Brooks frowned. "Nothing, man. Sorry." He turned and swiped his tablet. An image appeared on a second screen.

"She messed with your internal security cameras. She's damn good. But I did catch this image from an external camera. But this was it."

Ty leaned forward. It was a picture from the outside

of his warehouse. It was more shadow than anything, but he could just make out the impression of a tall, long body.

Her head and face were covered, so he had no idea what her hair or features looked like.

Who the hell was she?

"No prints," Brooks continued. "Like I said, she's good."

Yes, she was. This was no regular thief. She was well-trained, experienced, and after something.

He'd watched her scale the damn wall in his warehouse lab like a spider and climb out a tiny window.

On the main screen, he watched Team 52 make their landing somewhere in the desert. As they scooped up their billowing parachutes, he heard Axel making a joke about always hitting the spot.

Team 52 did dangerous, important work. There were a lot of bad people out there who wanted to get their hands on artifacts that had the power to help them do terrible things. The team took their job seriously.

Ty turned his attention back to the shadowy image of the woman. It was likely that she was one of those people.

He'd find her, and whatever the hell she was doing, he'd stop her.

CHAPTER TWO

Ty sipped his beer, glancing around the bar. They were out at Team 52's favorite place in Las Vegas —Griffin's Sports Bar and Grill.

They'd all been pumped after their training, and on the flight back into Las Vegas, everyone had agreed to a night out and a few beers.

Blair was playing pool with her man, Detective Luke MacKade. Axel was flirting with the bartender. Next to Ty, Lachlan sat with his woman, Rowan. The two of them were talking quietly and smiling. Next to them, Seth had his pregnant wife, January, sitting in his lap. The archeologist was glowing, and Seth looked pretty damned pleased with himself as he rubbed her belly. On the far side of them, Callie Kimura, sat sipping her wine.

The front door opened, and Smith and Kinsey arrived. It didn't take his genius IQ to see that Smith was pissed and Kinsey looked troubled.

Lachlan straightened. "Problem?"

"Someone was at our cabin," Smith ground out. "Searched the place."

The team went quiet.

"Your security system?" Seth asked.

"Disabled. And they drugged my fucking dog."

Callie gasped. "Is Hercules okay?"

Kinsey nodded. "That's why we're late. We took him to the emergency vet to get checked. He's fine."

"Anything missing?" Ty asked.

Smith shook his head.

"It was *her*," Ty said. "The same intruder who was at my place."

Lachlan's face turned unhappy. "Anyone else had any sign of uninvited visitors?"

Everyone shook their heads.

"What's going on?" Blair asked, pool cue still in hand. Luke stood behind her.

"Someone searched Smith and Kinsey's cabin," Lachlan said. "Your place secure?"

Luke shrugged a shoulder. "I had decent security, but since Blair moved in, we're in the middle of some upgrades."

Blair scowled. "Someone with skill could have gotten in without us knowing."

"She has the skill," Ty said.

"My place would be a challenge for the average person." Lachlan's golden gaze moved to Ty. "I want you to work with the team and upgrade everyone's personal security."

Ty nodded. "I've already started adding some enhancements." He paused. "We need to find this woman."

"Agreed," Blair said. "But tonight, we also need to blow off some steam. Everyone's been tense and moody."

Ty didn't fail to notice she looked at him as she said that.

Smith grabbed a beer off the bar. "I'm always tense and moody."

Kinsey snuggled into his side, smiling at the man. "Not always."

Instantly, Smith's gruff face softened.

God, Smith Creed in love. He'd been the last man Ty would have pegged to take the fall. Forcing himself to relax, Ty lifted his beer and took a large sip.

"And don't forget, tomorrow is my birthday and we're hitting that new club, Illumination." Her gaze locked on Ty. "*Everyone* is coming and that includes you."

"You just love subjecting me to masses of stupid people."

Blair raised a brow. "How do you know everyone there will be stupid?"

"One, because they're willingly at a nightclub, and two, I find most people stupid."

Blair smiled. "Ah, there's the sweet, friendly Ty we know and love."

He raised his drink to her.

Slowly, everyone started to unwind. Rowan started talking about some of her work at the local university.

"How are your projects going, Ty?" Seth asked.

Ty lifted his chin. "I'm working on several things. Had an ancient ceramic jar almost incinerate Nat today."

From nearby, Axel straightened. "What?"

"Flames shot out of this ancient jar from Iraq. Made a mess of my lab."

"Did she get hurt?" Axel's beer bottle cracked against the wooden bar. "I saw her this afternoon, she didn't mention anything..."

"She was fine. Spine of steel, that woman."

Axel looked like he wanted to storm out and find her.

"I also managed to open that box from the dig in India," Ty continued. "Contained a huge blue diamond."

January leaned forward. "Really? Sounds fascinating."

The conversation shifted beyond Ty's work, to the team dissecting their training jump.

Axel set his drink down. "I'm going to take a...ah, I'm heading to the restroom."

Ty cradled his beer and watched Blair sink an impossible shot at the pool table. She did a small victory dance, which had a smiling MacKade wrapping an arm around her. The detective pulled her in for a hard kiss.

Ty shook his head. The pair had been at each other's throats for at least a year. MacKade was Team 52's contact at the Las Vegas Metropolitan Police, and it often put him and Blair at odds. But during a recent, dangerous operation, the pair's enmity had morphed into something very different.

Lachlan and Rowan, Seth and January, Smith and Kinsey, and now Blair and MacKade... Ty tossed back some more beer. They were all taking some pretty big damn risks for this thing called love.

Ty's parents had a bloodless marriage. They weren't in love, but both came from the right backgrounds, and had a mutually beneficial partnership. On the side, they'd both had several love affairs—all messy and overemotional.

He shook his head. He'd learned young that getting emotionally involved was disordered, inefficient, and annoying. He watched Blair kiss the hell out of MacKade. But he had to admit his friends seemed to be making it work.

Ty had never found a woman he wanted to be around for very long. He usually found most women annoying, needy, and selfish. And always in his space. Demanding time and attention.

Blair appeared in front of him, her face flushed. "Where's Axel? I want to rub my pool brilliance in his face."

"Restroom." Ty frowned. "He's been gone a hell of a long time."

Blair stiffened, turning to glance back to the narrow corridor that led to the restrooms. Ty slid off his stool, unease rippling down his spine.

Lachlan leaned forward. "What's going on?"

"Axel's been gone too long," Ty said.

Lachlan set Rowan aside. "Stay here."

Ty, flanked by Blair and Lachlan, headed to the back of Griffin's. Ty opened the door to the Men's room. Lachlan checked it quickly and shook his head.

Blair checked the Woman's, and came out shaking her head.

"Where the hell did he go?" Lachlan murmured.

They moved farther down the corridor, that headed toward a back door into the alley at the back of the bar.

"Fuck." Lachlan leaped forward.

There was a small alcove to one side, stacked with old bar stools and brooms.

Axel was on his ass, slumped against the wall, eyes closed.

"Axel!" Blair dropped down beside him.

"Let me." Ty reached forward, checking the man's pulse. "He's alive." He patted Axel's cheek. "Axel? Axel?"

The man stirred, and when his brown eyes opened, they were unfocused.

His brow creased. "What...happened?"

"Hoping you could tell us?" Lachlan said.

Axel winced and pressed a hand to his head. "Fuck. There was a woman. Gorgeous woman. She'd just come out of the Ladies' and was flirting with me. Had the sexiest British accent, and all these curls. She wanted tips on places to go out in Vegas."

Ty felt a prickle of something along the back of his neck.

"Then she touched my face—" Axel reached up and touched his cheek. "Fuck. She did something. It knocked me out."

"Probably a fast-acting sedative absorbed through the skin," Ty said.

Axel patted his pockets, then cursed. "My keys are gone."

"It's her." Ty pushed to his feet. "The woman who's searching our places."

"She must be at my condo." Axel gripped onto Lachlan's arm as the team leader helped him up.

"Let's go," Ty said.

They hurried back to the bar to update the others.

Smith stood. "I'm coming."

"Me, too," said Seth.

Callie just rose and raised a dark eyebrow.

MacKade set his drink down. "Count me in."

"Go." January waved a hand. "Us ladies will stay here until you get back." Beside her, Rowan and Kinsey nodded.

Soon, all of Team 52 was striding out to their vehicles.

Axel still looked a little pale and unsteady. "Want a lift?" Ty asked.

"Thanks." He slid into the passenger seat of Ty's sporty Lexus.

As Ty pulled out onto the street, the tires squealed.

"I'm a fucking idiot," Axel muttered. "I'm former Delta Force. I can pick a fraud a mile away." He slammed a hand on the dash.

"I get the impression this woman is beyond good at what she does."

They reached Axel's condo and Ty found a parking spot out front. The others arrived just after them, and Axel retrieved his spare key from a lockbox.

After a short, tense ride in the elevator, they strode down the hall. Axel's building wasn't fancy, but it was neat and modern. He stopped at his door and unlocked it.

Everyone pulled out their handguns. Even though Ty was vibrating with impatience, he stayed at the back and let them do their thing.

They moved smoothly though the shadowed, two-bedroom condo. Axel's place was tidy, with a few typical bachelor additions—a huge television and a large, brown, suede couch—and a couple of surprising touches—several thriving houseplants, and some nice, modern lamps.

"Clear," Lachlan called out.

"Clear."

"Clear."

Axel flicked on the lights. "No one here."

Ty spied Axel's keys sitting on the granite kitchen counter. Other than that, the place looked untouched, and there was no female intruder.

Axel did the rounds, then came back, shaking his head. "Nothing missing."

"What does she want?" Lachlan's voice vibrated with anger.

That was the question Ty kept asking himself. He shoved his hands in the pockets of his jeans.

"Starting tomorrow, I want Brooks and Ty to check everyone's security systems," Lachlan ordered. "And starting tomorrow, we're going to do whatever the hell we have to in order to find this woman."

Ty smiled. *Game on.*

RIVER LEANED AGAINST HER RENTAL, drinking her takeout coffee.

There was a cold wind blowing. The heart of winter was over, but the air was crisp. Still, River liked the Las Vegas sunshine. It sure as hell beat London's dreary gray cloud cover.

She stared across the road and through the chain-link fence. On the other side of it was an ugly, squat, concrete building.

This was Team 52's Las Vegas headquarters, tucked into a corner of McCarran International Airport. They called it the Bunker.

It was an apt description. It was guarded by some tough security, and it would probably take a missile strike to break it open.

She could sneak into the airport grounds easily enough, but her recon told her she'd never be able to break into the Bunker without setting off some alarms. She took another sip of her caramel latte. She could sneak in. Maybe on the cleaning crew.

The phone in her pocket rang.

She pulled it out. "Yes."

"Progress report."

Her client. She heard the touch of the Middle-Eastern accent, even though he probably spoke better English than she did.

"I tracked the painting to Las Vegas. I'm running down leads."

"We paid you a lot of money, Ms. Elliott-Hall."

"I'm worth it." She took another sip of coffee. "I never fail."

"So I've been told. Don't make this job your first failure." The client ended the call.

With hundreds of millions of dollars at stake, the man had the right to be impatient.

River tucked the phone away and watched two black SUVs pull up in front of the Bunker. She didn't stiffen.

Just stayed relaxed and sipped her coffee. Like she belonged right where she was. She was dressed in yoga gear, with a zip-up sweater. She was also wearing a blonde wig.

She watched Lachlan Hunter exit the lead SUV.

The man had killer written all over him. Nothing in the way he moved suggested he had a prosthetic arm, but reports said he'd lost it on a mission as a Marine. She watched the rest of Team 52 get out of the vehicles.

The athletic blonde was Blair Mason. The woman with the straight black hair and Hawaiian features was the medic, Callie Kimura. The big guy was Smith Creed and the small blonde was his woman, Kinsey. The lean, dark-haired man with the scarred face was Seth Lynch.

She saw the sexy guy she'd drugged at the bar last night—Axel Diaz. Former Delta Force. She was lucky he'd been relaxed and had already had a beer, or he might not have fallen for her tourist ruse. He looked grumpy and pissed.

Her lips quirked. *Sorry, hot stuff.*

Then the big, African-American man slid out of the second SUV.

River felt a reluctant quiver in her belly.

She frowned. *He's just a man, River.* A mighty fine man, but just a man.

Ty Sampson had almost caught her in his place. She took in the broad shoulders and long legs. Even from a distance, she noted the sexy-as-hell goatee that covered his strong jaw.

From the dossier she'd read, Sampson was also scary

smart. He had a genius IQ and was good with his hands... Well, at least in his lab.

She watched as the team moved inside the concrete building. She didn't think Team 52 had anything to do with the theft of the *Salvator Mundi*.

River let out a frustrated breath.

If Team 52 hadn't taken it, that left her with no leads.

No leads made her job a hell of a lot harder.

She wouldn't fail. Her fingers curled around her cup until it crushed under the pressure.

She'd find a way.

Then she raised her head and her pulse jumped.

Ty Sampson was standing in the doorway of the Bunker...staring right at her through the chain-link fence.

They were too far away for him to get a good look at her, but she knew he was looking straight at her face.

Her heart thudded hard against her chest.

With unhurried movements, River opened her car door and slid inside. She started the Mercedes, forcing herself not to rush, even though every instinct in her body urged her to speed away.

She glided out onto the road, her heart still knocking in a steady rhythm. When she glanced back in the rearview mirror, she saw that Ty Sampson was still watching her.

CHAPTER THREE

"You look like you're being tortured."

Ty swiveled on his stool and scowled at Nat. They were celebrating Blair's birthday and he'd been assured that this nightclub was Las Vegas' hottest new club. He couldn't even remember what its pretentious, trendy name was.

"Are you having fun?" he yelled against the loud music.

Nat smiled and lifted a fluted glass filled with some frothy drink. "It's a party, Ty. You're supposed to have fun."

He grunted, and with a roll of her eyes, Nat strolled toward the gang standing around a high table. He wasn't in the mood for celebrating. He'd spent the day in the lab and bothering Brooks. They'd had no luck tracking down the woman. There'd been no prints at Axel's place. No image of her on Griffin's security cameras. Nothing.

Yesterday, Ty had seen a woman watching the

Bunker. She'd been a blonde, but something about her had pinged and had his instincts flaring. Had it been her?

Lights from the dance floor strobed in his eyes and he took a sip of his drink. He hated nightclubs. They were usually too dark, or too bright, the music too loud, and there were too many people.

He turned and saw Blair laughing, her head thrown back. She and Callie were on the dance floor, bopping to the music. A few brave men tried to approach them, but neither woman needed any protection. They could probably take down everyone on the dance floor in sixty seconds flat. They dispatched their would-be suitors fairly quickly.

The rest of the team was nursing their drinks and chatting. Nat and Kinsey stood off to the side, talking earnestly about something. Lachlan had an arm around Rowan, talking with Seth, Smith, and Axel.

"Want to dance?"

Ty turned his head. A stacked blonde was standing in front of him. She wore a tiny dress in gleaming pink, her hair was a mass of artfully done curls, and her breasts defied gravity.

"Hell, no," he said.

The woman blinked, clearly not used to that response. "We'd have a good time."

"I don't think so."

Her lips tipped down in a scowl. "Fine, then." She swiveled on her high heels and walked away.

"You'll be single forever, *mi amigo*," Axel said. "Especially if you keep turning away goods like that."

"I'd be perfectly fine with being single forever. I don't

need someone in my way, messing up my things, wanting attention."

Axel laughed. "You'll be old and lonely."

"Are you going to settle down?"

The man froze. "There's too much variety to enjoy." His dark gaze flicked to the dance floor.

Ty glanced in the same direction, and saw that Nat and Kinsey had joined Blair and Callie on the dance floor.

"For a former Delta Force operator, you're a terrible liar," Ty said.

"Shut up. I'm going to get another drink." Axel stalked off.

As Axel headed for the bar, Ty moved over to a railing that looked down to a second dance floor below. He leaned over, scanning the heaving crowd as the lights strobed.

He couldn't think of anything worse than being pressed up against that swelling mass of sweating people.

Then he felt a prickle on the back of his neck.

For a few moments, he didn't move, just kept looking down at the churning mass of humanity below. Then, slowly, he turned his head.

Out of the shadows, a woman sauntered through the crowd. She walked like she was royalty, and the crowd parted for her.

She was gorgeous, her long, lithe body sheathed in a shimmering gold dress that looked like liquid covering her. She had long, long legs, glossy dark skin, and a long fall of straight, black hair.

Her eyes met his—they were a tawny, light brown. She held a fancy looking cocktail in one hand.

"This railing taken?" she asked.

"No." He heard the crisp British accent in her voice.

She leaned against the rail. "You look like you'd rather be doing your taxes than be here."

"I like doing my taxes." He sipped his beer.

She laughed. A lovely sound he felt in his gut.

Her hair was straight, but it was *her*. He was sure of it.

"So, you hate having fun?" A faint smile flirted on perfectly formed lips.

She was beautiful. Ty wasn't a man who noticed looks first. He almost always admired brains and wit before anything else.

But something about this woman made it hard to look away. Her beauty, the confidence she exuded, the glint in her eye.

"Mostly, I just dislike people," he said.

Now she laughed—full-bodied and sexy. "At least you're honest."

"I'm always honest." He tilted his head. "It's a good quality to have, don't you think?"

She shrugged a slender shoulder. "I'd rate a few others higher."

Right. Like breaking and entering, and sedating people. "Want to find a quiet corner where we can actually hear each other talk?"

Her smile widened. "I'd like that." She took a sip of her drink. "I take it I'm not annoying you?"

"Not yet."

She laughed again, and this time he thought he saw a faint look of surprise in her eyes. Those unique light brown eyes were gorgeous.

"Okay then, Mr. Antisocial," she said. "Lead the way."

Ty grabbed her hand. He wasn't letting her out of his sight.

Electricity tingled on his fingers and skated up his arm. He heard the woman gasp, and his fingers flexed on hers.

He pulled her a little closer. She smelled like spice and wood.

And she was all his now.

Ty tugged her deeper into the crowd.

———

BLOODY HELL, he smelled good.

River was pressed way too close to Ty Sampson. She felt the heat pumping off his big body, along with the delicious aftershave he wore.

He glanced her way, and her gaze locked with his dark eyes. Then she looked lower, to the sexy shape of his lips framed by that hot goatee.

She turned her head, looking at the crowd. *Stay focused on the job, River.* She wasn't used to feeling desire curling in her belly, or heat prickling over her skin.

She had sex, when she had the time. Anonymous pickups. But not on a job. Never ever.

He led her over to a table with some low chairs, in a quieter corner of the club. He held out a chair for her and she sat. Then he grabbed another chair and pulled it up close to hers.

"So, you're not from Vegas," he said.

She arched a brow. "What gave me away?"

"The sexy accent."

River licked her lips. "You're the one with the accent, not me." She leaned forward, making sure her neckline was on display. "So, what do you do when you're not out at fancy nightclubs, not enjoying yourself?"

His gaze didn't leave her face. "I invent things."

"Do you? So, you're a mad scientist."

His teeth were white against his dark skin. "Something like that. And you?"

"I'm in acquisitions. I travel a lot."

He just stared at her, like he could see into her head. "You like it?"

She nodded. "I'm good at it. I like being the best."

"Me, too."

They stared at each other and she felt the hum between them.

"There's something about winning that is a lovely fuck you to the rest of the world." Shit, why had she said that?

He leaned closer, cradling his hands between his knees. "Who you sending that message to?"

"Shitty family." She shrugged a shoulder. "Who else? I'm a walking cliché with daddy issues."

Shit. Stop talking, River.

Ty lifted a broad shoulder. "My parents never really cared enough for me to bother giving them a fuck you."

There was a coolness in his voice that made her shiver. "So, you have daddy *and* mommy issues."

"No. They don't factor for me. I see them occasionally, and send my mother flowers for her birthday. That's it."

River thought it sounded lonely and cold. She shook her glass, making the ice tinkle. She'd loved her mother, and they'd been close until Celeste Elliot had died of cancer. River's father...was a complicated issue. Her stomach curdled at the thought of him.

"What's your name?" Ty asked.

She glanced at him over the rim of her glass. "How about we keep the mystery alive and leave names out of it. Would you like to dance?"

"Hell, no." He leaned closer. "I don't dance. But what I really want is to know why you snuck into my warehouse and my friends' cabin, and drugged my friend at the bar last night."

River froze. She went to move, but his big hand whipped out and landed on hers. He pressed it toward her other wrist and before she knew it, she found her wrists bound with a cable tie.

Anger roared through her. Dammit, he'd outsmarted her.

She tried to remember the last time that had happened. She tilted her head. *Never.*

She looked at his face. The smug bastard smiled at her. Jack would be shaking his head at her right now.

"You're not winning, today, Miss Mystery."

She glanced at her bound wrists. "This won't stop me."

"I made this tie. It's not ordinary plastic. You can't cut through it without a saw."

River leaned back and moving fast, she shifted to jam her high heel between his legs.

He matched her speed, trapping her leg between his with his powerful thighs.

She bit back a curse.

He rose and grabbed her arms, crowding her body with his. She was sure to anyone looking, it appeared they were flirting.

Ty leaned down until his warm lips brushed her ear. "Now," he drawled. "We're going somewhere quiet to have a little chat."

River tossed her head back, boldly meeting his gaze. "Okay, Mr. Scientist. You want to chat, we'll chat."

Meanwhile, River would bide her time until she could even the score.

CHAPTER FOUR

Ty paced the interrogation room at the Bunker. Nearby, Lachlan and Seth were watching him.

The others had stayed at the nightclub to keep the party going, although Blair had argued because she'd wanted to come. Blair rarely liked to miss out on a fight.

Lachlan leaned against the wall, his arms crossed over his chest. Seth sat on a backward-turned chair, his arms resting along the back.

Seth was in charge of questioning their guest. But so far, the woman was refusing to talk.

The woman was tied to a chair in the center of the cement-walled room. She looked like she didn't have a care in the world.

Her light-brown gaze lifted and met Ty's. She raised her stubborn chin another inch.

Defiant, fucking gorgeous, and frustrating as hell.

"I'm not going to tell you anything," she drawled.

And overconfident.

Screw this. Ty stomped over to a cabinet in the corner of the room, unlocked it, and started to sort through the few things he kept at the Bunker. He pulled out a small case.

"Ty…" Lachlan said, a warning in his voice.

Their guest stiffened.

Ty opened the case and pulled out a syringe and a small vial of fluid. He pushed the needle into the top of the vial, tipped it up, and filled the syringe. "It's a new mix I put together. It won't hurt her."

He turned and saw her watching him with a laser focus. He stalked toward her and she tensed even more.

"You'll just feel a little sting," he said.

"Bastard."

Ty expertly injected her in the top of her toned arm. "I often am."

"What's it do?" she bit out.

"This'll loosen your lips a little."

She jerked against the ties binding her to the chair.

"Ty's grumpy on a good day, doesn't pay to piss him off," Seth said.

"You won't get away with this." She made a hissing sound. "I'll even the score."

Anger seethed in her eyes and she glared at Ty. Man, she really hated losing.

"You broke into my place and then gave me the slip," Ty said. "That's one point to you. Now I've caught you, and we'll get some answers. I'd say we're even."

"You just injected me with a *drug*." Her glare was hot enough to strip paint. "I'll get payback for that."

Gripping the arms of her chair, he leaned down, their faces close. "Bring it, Ms. Mystery."

The minutes ticked by and he saw her face slowly start to relax. The drug was working its way into her system. He nodded at Seth and stepped back.

"Who are you?" Seth said.

Her face twisted. "Screw you."

Seth glanced at Ty. "My guess is she's trained to withstand the effects of some drugs."

The man would know, since he was a former CIA agent.

"And torture," she added.

Ty raised a brow. Hell, they weren't going to torture her. A part of him hated that she thought that, which annoyed the hell out of him. "She can't withstand this."

"So, you're trained and British," Seth continued. "I'm guessing MI6."

She turned to look at the wall. "I'm not MI6."

Seth smiled. "But you used to be. What's your name?"

She struggled against her bindings and made a low growling sound. "Petunia."

Lachlan rolled his eyes.

"Why are you after Team 52?" Seth persisted.

"I'm not."

"Why did you break into our places?"

"For my job." She kept struggling. "I'm looking for something."

"What?" Ty asked.

She looked at him, her eyes a little cloudy now. "A...painting."

Now they were getting somewhere.

"And you thought we had it?" Lachlan asked.

"Yes. You have a reputation for collecting...certain artifacts."

So, there was something unique about this painting. Ty wondered what exactly. "What is the painting?"

She was fighting the drug's effects, gritting her teeth. Ty hadn't seen anyone withstand this long. "The *Salvator Mundi.*"

He looked at Lachlan and Seth. They both shrugged. Ty had never heard of it, but he wasn't an art aficionado.

"She's fighting the drug hard," Seth noted.

Ty could see perspiration beading on her brow. He crouched beside her and pressed his fingers to her neck. She tried to jerk away.

"Her pulse rate is a little elevated."

"Give her a break," Lachlan said. "Let's connect with Brooks and find out what this painting is."

Ty rose and nodded.

As the other two walked out of the room, Ty moved over to a side table and lifted a jug. He poured a glass of water. He moved back to her, holding the glass up to her lips.

She glared at him, but took a sip.

"We won't hurt you," he said.

She looked away, staring resolutely at the wall again.

Ty pressed a finger under her chin and lifted it up. "What's your name?"

She just glared at him. "I know all about you and your team, Dr. Tyler Mitchell Sampson. I know you're the heir to the Sampson Finance fortune. Your parents are wealthy, but distant. Your father is a finance whiz, and your mother is a successful lawyer. You joined DARPA after you collected an impressive set of degrees from various top colleges. You have a genius IQ."

"What's your name?"

She was silent for a second, her jaw tight from grinding her teeth together. "River."

"There, that wasn't too hard." *River*. He rolled the name around in his head. "Unique. Suits you."

Her brow wrinkled, and it made her look cute and confused.

Ty gave her another sip of water. "Now, behave River."

As he went to find Lachlan and Seth, he felt her scowl like a laser beam on his back. In the main room of the Bunker, he found the men standing at Kinsey's desk, looking at a computer monitor. Brooks' face was on the screen.

"Her name is River," Ty said.

Seth arched a brow. "She just told you that? Or did you have to pull out some of her teeth or fingernails?"

Ty shot the man a look.

Lachlan jerked his head. "Brooks was going to tell us about the painting."

Brooks nudged his glasses up and tapped on his tablet. "I'm pissed I'm missing Blair's party."

"There'll be another party," Lachlan said. "The *Salvator Mundi*?"

"Got it." Brooks let out a whistle.

"What?" Ty demanded, leaning forward.

"The painting was recently discovered. It's been

around for a long time, but no one actually knew who'd painted it. Last year, it was determined that it was painted by Leonardo da Vinci."

"Fuck," Lachlan bit out.

Ty grimaced, sharing the sentiment. They had several da Vinci artifacts locked in secure storage at Area 52. The man had been ahead of his time, and had access to a lot of ancient knowledge.

Most of his artifacts were powerful and dangerous.

"Over the years," Brooks continued, "well-meaning people had done 'restoration' work to the *Salvator Mundi*. Essentially, they'd overpainted it and ruined it. It was always believed to be a copy of Leonardo's long-lost original. Once those layers were removed, it was authenticated as a da Vinci. It was purchased by a prince, on behalf of Abu Dhabi's Department of Culture and Tourism, and to be displayed at the Louvre Abu Dhabi—"

"There's a Louvre in Abu Dhabi?" Lachlan asked.

"Yes," Brooks confirmed. "It was a joint project between France and Abu Dhabi. The *Salvator Mundi* was going to be the jewel in the museum's crown after they purchased the painting for —" Brooks paused dramatically.

"Brooks," Lachlan said.

"Four hundred and fifty million dollars."

"Hell." Seth leaned back.

A muscle in Lachlan's jaw ticked.

Ty let out a low whistle.

"But?" Lachlan asked. "There's always a but."

"But nothing." Brooks leaned closer to the screen.

"The museum is doing their own restoration on the painting, and it'll be on display soon."

A picture of the painting came on the screen, and Ty frowned. It looked like Jesus holding a glass orb in his hand. It wasn't the prettiest picture he'd even seen. He didn't see anything particularly special about the painting.

"This is the latest image I can find of it, but my guess is that it might look a little different if they've done more restoration on it," Brooks said. "*Salvator Mundi* means 'savior of the world.' The painting shows Christ making the sign of the cross with one hand, and holding a crystal orb—the celestial sphere of the heavens —in his other."

Lachlan grunted.

"Wait." Brooks' voice took on an excited edge. "I just found some articles." He looked up. "Guys, the painting was supposed to have gone on display at the museum *months* ago. The Louvre Abu Dhabi canceled the opening."

"Go on," Lachlan said.

"And then nothing. It's not on display, and the museum won't respond to questions about it, or give a date of when it might be put on display."

"Stolen," Ty said.

"Maybe," Brooks said. "Maybe the restoration work is taking longer than they thought." He shrugged his broad shoulders. "I wouldn't want to screw up a painting worth that much."

"Maybe they realized it wasn't a da Vinci," Seth suggested.

Ty looked toward the closed door of the room holding River. "Stolen."

Lachlan pressed his hands to the desk and leaned forward. "Brooks, find out if there is anything special about this painting." Then the Team 52 leader looked at Ty. "Let's talk to our guest, and see if she knows why this painting is so important."

They swiveled, and Ty followed Lachlan into the room.

Then he heard Lachlan curse.

"Hell," Seth muttered.

Pulse jumping, Ty stepped around Lachlan, then muttered his own curse.

The chair was empty.

He looked up and saw that the tiny window at the top of the wall, not big enough for a man to get through, was open.

She'd escaped out that tiny window wearing a dress and high heels. And she still had her hands zip-tied together. She'd broken the arms off the chair to get free.

Ty walked over and kicked the broken chair. "Fuck."

PISSED AS HELL, River quickly jogged toward the airport fence. Her head was fuzzy and she was thirsty.

Where she could, she stayed in the shadows. There was a cool wind blowing, and she was cold as hell. She'd tried to get the zip ties off, but as the grumpy, sexy scientist had promised, she couldn't budge them.

She found a small hole in the chain-link fence. A few

good, solid kicks and it was large enough for her to crawl through. She heard fabric rip and sighed. There went her very expensive dress.

On the other side of the fence, she hurried toward the road and tripped. Her curses were ripe and colorful. While she was on her knees, she heard an SUV start in the distance and turned her head.

An SUV zipped away from the Bunker, headlights spearing through the darkness.

River dropped flat on the ground, hoping she was hidden enough by the scraggly grass.

The SUV pulled out onto the road. It wasn't driving fast, and she knew they were searching for her.

She needed to get back to the hotel room she'd rented under an alias. It was in a shitty hotel off the Strip, but there, she could regroup.

The SUV finally disappeared into the darkness, and she blew out a breath. Her dress was damp and she was starting to shiver. She needed a change of clothes.

She rose and jogged along the road.

Ahead, she saw a large warehouse building with an orange-and-white sign. *Perfect.*

With her hands tied, it took a few minutes for her to bypass the security and break into a back door of the Home Depot. Inside, her steps echoed through the cavernous space. She walked down a couple of aisles before she found the saws.

Awkwardly, she maneuvered the saw up against the zip tie, and prayed that she wouldn't lose a finger. She started sawing through the tough plastic.

Finally, the tie fell off her wrists. *Thank God.*

River shook her arms, working the aches out. Turning, she marched through the store, collecting what she needed. She ditched the dress and pulled on some work pants, a thick, plaid shirt, a suede coat, and then boots. The boots were too big, but an extra pair of socks helped.

She straightened, feeling better already. She rocked workman chic.

At the front registers, she pulled out some cash from the small emergency stash she kept hidden in her bra. She tucked the notes beneath the edge of one register. It was more than enough to cover what she'd taken.

Then she headed out. It was still dark as she started walking back toward the Strip. The casinos rose up in the distance like a beacon. It wasn't long before she managed to flag down a cab and slid into the back seat.

"Desert Star Inn."

The driver glanced at her in the rear-view mirror. She saw his eyebrows wing up.

"You sure?"

"Yes." She turned to look out the window.

She heard him mutter something about bed bugs. He probably wasn't lying. They headed towards the shining lights of the Strip.

River leaned back against the seat. Team 52 didn't have the painting. They were a dead-end.

Knowing that, she wished she'd never gained their attention. She tapped her fingers on her knee. Hopefully, their interest in her and the painting would die now.

She caught her reflection in the window, thinking of Ty Sampson's dark gaze. She probably wasn't going to be that lucky.

She pushed Dr. Grumpy's face out of her head. She needed to find the *Salvator Mundi* and get out of town.

She had to focus on her only other lead, and that was Chadwick Alton. It was too much of a coincidence that the wealthy casino owner's jet had flown from Abu Dhabi to Las Vegas just hours after the painting went missing. Despite the painting not being in his gallery at the Constellation, it had to be him.

Alton. Her hands clenched on her thighs. Maybe she just wanted it to be him. The man touted his business skills in hotels and casinos, but the behind-the-scenes truth was that the aging billionaire had his sticky fingers in the arms trade, selling weapons and military technology.

And one of those deals had killed MI6 agent Jack Rothwell.

Do the job, River. Never get emotional. Jack's voice in her head.

Right. Next up, check Alton's huge mansion out in Summerlin, and then take a look in the penthouse in the city he used to cheat on his wife.

Men, especially wealthy men, were all the same. They took what they wanted and damn the consequences.

River shook her head. That was her father to a *T*. Henry loved her, in his own way. Since she was a little girl, he'd always invited her to his fancy estate outside London to spend time with his family. She got to see her half-brothers, who were way older than her, on occasion. They were mostly bemused by the illegitimate half-sister they'd inherited. They'd never been mean to her, but were never welcoming, either.

And her father's wife...well, River could hardly blame Lady Caroline for her less-than-warm demeanor. It couldn't have been easy, when your husband tried to insert his illegitimate child from an affair into your life and family.

River closed her eyes. Damn, she still felt a bit groggy from the drug. It was a relief when the cab finally pulled up in front of the tired, worn façade of her hotel. She climbed out, not that excited to return to her dingy room that smelled of cigarette smoke and sweat.

In her head, she was already formulating her plan to break into Alton's mega mansion.

The attack came fast.

Four men dressed in black rushed at her.

Fucking hell. River dodged, blocking punches. She ducked, spun, and kicked out. Her front kick slammed into one man, who went flying. She dodged another kick by an inch.

Shit. She was sluggish from the drug.

The fight was fast and brutal. The three men left standing converged. She managed to kick and punch one man, then leaped into the air, wrapping her legs around his neck.

He cried out and she twisted her body. They crashed onto the sidewalk. She heard his elbow hit the concrete and a bone snap. He yelped.

River leaped up, but two more rushed at her.

She dodged blows, but then one landed a fist in her belly.

Damn, that hurt. Pain vibrated through her, and she sucked in a harsh breath. Regrouping, she kicked again. She sent one big asshole slamming into a car and she smiled.

Then two beefy arms wrapped around her from behind. She tensed, then felt the sharp sting of a knife at her side. *Shit.*

"You weren't supposed to cut her," a man muttered.

"Bitch broke Freddy's arm."

The knife sliced through her clothes and cut her skin. She felt the seep of blood. Then the man shoved her away.

River staggered away, pressing her hand against the bleeding wound.

"Mr. Alton doesn't like people who break into his art gallery," the man holding the knife said.

Fuck. How the hell did Alton know who she was?

The man held out his other hand and she saw a crumpled photo printout. It was a picture of her at the Constellation Casino. She was walking out of the staff corridor.

Damn, she knew all the casinos had top-notch facial recognition systems.

"This is a warning," the man said. "Stay away from Mr. Alton and his properties."

The man stepped back, and suddenly, River's legs turned to jelly. She pressed a hand to the wall of the hotel, watching the four goons head off. One was cradling his arm and glaring at her.

"You won't get another warning," the man with the broken arm called back.

Yeah, yeah. She pressed harder on her side and winced. Blood was soaking into her clothes and her side burned.

Dizziness washed over River, and when she looked up, she could practically feel the strength draining out of her. Damn, the cut was deeper than she'd initially thought.

It took her a really long time to push herself off the wall. Nausea rose and she breathed through her nose. *Don't be sick, River, and don't pass out.*

She was alone. She knew no one in Las Vegas. She could bleed out here on this shitty Las Vegas side street, and no one would care.

Leaning on the wall again, uncaring that she was leaving a smear of blood behind, she staggered down the street.

She wasn't sure where she was going, but she wasn't going to bloody well die today.

CHAPTER FIVE

T y drove back toward his warehouse, frustration eating at his gut. He smacked his hand against the steering wheel.

Damn. She'd gotten away. They'd looked for her everywhere, and there'd been no sign of her.

She was sneaky, talented, and smart.

He turned into the back alley leading to the rear of his warehouse. As he got close, he touched a button on his dash. "Computer, open warehouse rear roller door."

Then his Lexus' headlights flashed on something slumped against the back wall of his place.

He frowned. Then he realized it wasn't something, but *someone.*

Ty slammed on the brakes and threw open his door.

He rushed over and saw instantly that it was River. Her chin was on her chest, her legs stretched out in front of her. She was wearing jeans, a red plaid shirt, brown jacket, and bulky boots.

"River?" He dropped to his knees beside her.

Her eyelids lifted, and light-brown eyes blinked up at him.

"Ty... Didn't know...where else to go."

Her voice was slurred and he touched her neck. Her pulse was a little thready. He patted her down, pulling open the bulky jacket.

The plaid beneath was wet and soaked with blood.

"Fuck." He scooped her up and she let out a low moan.

"Hurts."

"I know, baby. Hang in there."

He rushed to the now-open roller door and strode inside. The back part of his warehouse was where he parked his car, then it opened into his home laboratory.

"Computer, lights."

Light flooded the space. Long benches filled most of the lab, and he quickly laid her out on an empty bench. He tore through his drawers and pulled out some fresh gauze. He shoved up the plaid shirt and when he saw the knife wound, he scowled. He pressed the gauze against the injury.

"Hold that." He moved her hand to hold the wadded fabric in place.

Moving fast, he raced back outside and drove his car in. At the roller door, he checked the alleyway.

There was no sign of anyone.

"Computer, close roller door and activate security system."

The roller door rumbled as it started to close. When he got back to River, he saw she hadn't moved. He snapped on some gloves and pulled out his heavy-duty first aid kit.

Her head turned toward him, her cheeks pale beneath her dark skin. He pulled out some scissors and started cutting her jacket and shirt off.

"Am I annoying you yet?" she murmured.

"You've been a pain in my ass from the first moment I laid eyes on you."

She made a sound. "I have that effect on people. And in England, we'd say pain in the *arse*."

He snorted. "Don't think you're special. Everybody annoys me." Her belly was flat and toned, and her full breasts were encased in a simple black bra. He checked the ugly gash from the knife and frowned. "So, you managed to get yourself stabbed. Perfect way to top off a shitty night."

"I know. Bloody inconsiderate of me."

He probed the wound gently. "What happened?"

"Bad guys. Warning." Her eyes closed.

Ty pulled out some painkillers and antibiotics. He carefully injected her. He assumed that her tetanus shot was up to date, considering her line of work.

"Happens," she muttered.

"Your job sucks."

"Maybe," she agreed.

He started cleaning the wound. He heard her hiss out a breath, but other than that, she stayed still and silent.

"You need a couple of stiches."

"Figured."

Ty took his time stitching her wound. "You're lucky it

wasn't too deep. If they'd hit something vital, you wouldn't have made it here."

She made a sound, and he wasn't sure if she was agreeing or not.

He held up a tube. "This cream is a special formulation of mine. It'll quicken your rate of healing."

"Really?"

"Yep. Got my hands on the makeup of a miracle salve found in the Amazon jungle. I've managed to replicate some of its properties."

He smoothed some of the cream over the wound, then pressed a bandage over the top. It looked stark against her dark skin. "There."

When he lifted his gaze, he saw she was watching him. Without stopping to think why, he reached up and pushed her dark hair off her face.

"This is usually curly, right?" He fingered the strands.

She nodded. "I like to mix up the styles. Although straightening it can be a process."

"I'd like to see it curly."

She blinked. "You have a better bedside manner than I'd guessed."

"This is only for you. Ask my team, they bitch about my lack of empathy all the time."

Her lips quirked, her eyes fluttering closed.

"So—" he pulled a stool over and sat "—the *Salvator Mundi* was stolen from the Louvre Abu Dhabi."

Those eyes blinked open. "You've been busy."

"Who took it?"

"If I knew, I wouldn't have been breaking into your

place." She sighed. "I have no leads, except one that led me to Las Vegas. I knew this was Team 52's stomping ground, I'd heard what you guys did, and figured it was worth seeing if you had the painting."

"What's special about the *Salvator Mundi*?"

Her eyelids flickered closed. "You're way too handsome for a scientist." Her voice was slurred with fatigue.

Ty shook his head. He took in her half-naked form and decided he needed to find her a shirt. He lifted her wrist and checked her pulse again. She had very delicate wrists for such a tough woman.

"We could help you," he said.

Eyes still closed, she shook her head. "And have Team 52 snatch the painting and take over? Uh-uh, no way. This is *my* job."

Then she promptly passed out.

Ty finished up and stared at her face. Her color was better and her wound was clean. He blew out a breath, then reached out and touched her hair again.

He pulled his gloves off and then slid his arms under her. When he lifted her against his chest, she snuggled in against him. He paused, wondering why instead of feeling irritated, he liked the weight of her. With a shake of his head, he walked toward the bedrooms.

He had a guest room, but he didn't stop to question why he set her down on his bed. Next, he set to work stripping the work pants off her long legs. She stirred, rolling onto her uninjured side, and giving him a view of a mighty fine ass in tiny black panties.

Gritting his teeth, he went to his closet and grabbed a

T-shirt. He contemplated putting it on her, but he might jostle her injury. *Shit*. He tossed the shirt aside.

He knew he should call Lachlan. But it was late—or early, depending on your perspective—and it had been a long night. She wasn't going anywhere right now.

Exhaustion tugged at him. Ty wasn't ashamed to admit he really liked his sleep. He needed good quality sleep to keep his mind sharp and do his job well. Nat had told him numerous times that he was especially unbearable when he was tired.

Ty took his time washing up and getting dressed for bed. He pulled on his favorite, old, gray sweatpants. Then he lay down beside River.

River—a prickly, dangerous, and likely MI6-trained mystery woman.

She stirred mumbling something that included his name. Then she burrowed into his side.

"Computer, turn off bedroom lights."

Ty wrapped an arm around her and stared at the ceiling. Strangely, it didn't take him long to fall asleep.

RIVER WOKE BESIDE A MAN.

Tensing, she rolled over. Waking up with someone in her bed was a rare occurrence. It *never* happened.

She took in dark skin and the heat of a big, hard body.

She licked her lips. *Well.* A shirtless Ty Sampson was something to behold.

Everything inside River flared to painful life. *Oh, boy.*

She lifted a hand. *Don't do it, River. Just get up and get out.*

Instead, she reached out and touched him. Firm, warm skin.

She sucked in a breath. He'd woken her a few hours ago to check on her and give her more pain meds. She could count on one hand how many times someone had tended her wounds and looked after her through her life.

Her mother had been a busy, working, single mother. There hadn't been much time for coddling. And her father hadn't ever been around for the small stuff.

River stretched her side carefully. It felt pretty good.

Unconsciously, she stroked Ty's abdomen again. The man clearly got out of the lab and into the gym a lot.

Suddenly, a big hand touched hers. She tried to jerk away, but his fingers closed over hers, holding her hand pressed flat against his abs.

She looked up at him. That sexy goatee was the perfect frame for his gorgeous lips. He was just too damn tempting.

"How you feeling?" His voice was deep and sleepy.

"Fine. Thanks."

They kept staring at each other. God, she felt like there was a wire linking them. Again, her internal alarm told her to get away, and instead, she found herself moving closer.

Their faces were only inches apart. His body was tense beneath hers.

She cleared her throat. "Thanks for saving my life, Ty." She closed the distance and pressed her mouth to his.

His lips parted and a deep groan rumbled through him. His hand slid into her hair and at first, the kiss was slow, deep, and thorough. Exactly what she expected of this man.

But it didn't stay that way.

It was like dry tinder catching fire. The flames roared, and his hand clenched in her hair. She leaned in, stroking her tongue against his. Bloody hell, he tasted good. He took over, and she tried to get control back. But his tongue thrust into her mouth, and suddenly River didn't want to do anything except be ravished.

Her hands clenched on his skin, and the kiss went on and on. She pressed against him, drawing in the taste and feel of him.

Finally, he raised his head. His breathing was uneven. "River—"

"Wow." She shook her head. Her heart was hammering in her chest. "That... Got out of hand."

He watched her with dark eyes, like a big, vigilant panther. "I take it you're feeling better."

"Oh, yeah." Except she was a flaming mass of desire.

"You going to let me help you now?"

She sat up, pulling away from him. "I don't need help."

He made an angry sound. "You did last night."

River slid off the bed. Hell, she was only in her underwear. She looked around and had vague recollections of him undressing her. *Damn.*

"River, listen to me—"

"Look, Ty." She spun to face him. "It's best if you just forget about me and the *Salvator Mundi*."

He sat up on the pillows, shoving one behind his back. For a second, River was distracted by the flex of the muscles in his stomach. *God*. Her gaze drifted down. She wanted to lick him all over. She eyed the sheet pooled in his lap, and wanted to know exactly what it was covering. *Damn him for being so delectable.*

Don't lose your head, River. That was a lesson her father liked to repeat to her. Although he rarely followed it himself—especially when beautiful women were involved.

River looked around and spotted some clothes tossed on an armchair in the corner. At some stage, Ty had discarded a suit. She grabbed the white shirt and pulled it over her head. It was too big, and one breath warned her it held his very delicious and distracting scent.

She saw the dark tie on top of his jacket. She picked it up, running the silky fabric through her fingers.

"Pretty sure I can't forget you." Ty's voice was a deep purr. "Especially when you're standing in my bedroom and only wearing my shirt."

She turned to face him. "Try harder."

"River, I'm not letting you leave. I'm going to call Lachlan and we'll all talk. You tell us everything, including if the *Salvator Mundi* is dangerous. Then Team 52 can help you."

She shook her head. "You'll take over and then you'll lock the painting away." And there went her job and her reputation. "No way."

River had to get this done herself. Alone. That was always the best and the only way she knew.

She sauntered over to the bed, watching his gaze drop to her bare legs. "You should go back to your lab, Ty."

She pressed one knee to the covers and leaned over him. Once again she ignored her internal alarm as it screeched at her. One last taste wouldn't matter. She kissed him again. This kiss softer, slower.

"I could kiss you all day," he growled against her lips.

Startled, she looked into his eyes. No one had ever said that to her before.

Before he could weaken her resolve, River quickly moved her hands, looping the tie around his wrists.

"What the fuck?" He jerked upright.

But River had already tied his wrists to the carved wooden headboard. She tied a knot and cinched it in tight. She checked the knot. Yep, he wouldn't get loose any time soon.

She sat back. "I'm sorry."

"River." He gave the tie a hard yank.

She walked over to his closet. She pulled out some of his clothes, which were way too big for her, but they'd do until she could get to her own gear.

"I have to go."

"Fuck." He threw himself back against the pillows. "You are the most distrusting woman I've ever met."

She turned and cocked a hip. "Oh, and you're the king of being trusting and depending on others? I know you don't have long-term relationships. You've already admitted to me that you basically dislike people. And you're moody and grumpy."

He glared at her, looking way too sexy tied to the bed. It gave her far too many ideas.

River yanked on a pair of his jeans. "Your parents fucked you up. I get it."

"I'm not ruled by my past or my parents," he bit out.

"We all are." She shrugged. "Just roll with it."

"River, untie me."

"I can't." She cinched the jeans in with a belt. Moving back to the bed, she leaned over him again, pressing one hand to his hard chest. "I am sorry."

She pressed a kiss to his temple and heard him groan in frustration.

Then she pulled back. She started out of the room.

"I'll find you," he said.

She glanced back over her shoulder and shot him a smile. "No, you won't."

Besides, the men in her life never stuck around. Eventually, everyone left and you realized you never really had them.

Alone was the only guaranteed way to stay safe and whole.

"Goodbye, Ty." She flicked him a two-fingered salute.

Surprisingly, for the first time in her life, River found it hard to walk away.

CHAPTER SIX

When Lachlan and Seth walked into his bedroom, Ty was still tied up and pissed as hell. He was also worried about River, but he wasn't going to admit to that.

He'd managed to use the voice activation on his system to call Lachlan. Seth was trying hard not to laugh, and Lachlan just looked grim.

"What happened?" Lachlan asked.

"River was here. Found her slumped outside my place. She'd been stabbed."

"And yet she still tied you up," Seth said. "To your bed."

"Fuck you, Lynch," Ty grumbled.

Lachlan pulled a knife off his belt, reached over the bed, and sliced through the tie.

Ty rubbed his wrists. "Goons belonging to some casino owner attacked her. They'd managed to get a snap of her face when she broke into his art gallery looking for the stolen painting."

Lachlan shoved his knife away. "She confirmed the *Salvator Mundi* was stolen?"

Ty nodded.

"Shit." Seth crossed his arms. "And did she share what's so special about it?"

Ty shook his head. "She wouldn't say." He stood and strode over to find a T-shirt. "We need to find her and the painting."

"How the hell are we going to find her?" Seth said. "If she's MI6, she's in the wind."

"I put a tracker on her," Ty said.

"What?" Lachlan's brow creased.

Seth smiled. "She know?"

"Hell, no." And Ty knew River would be spitting mad when she found out he'd pressed a tiny microdot on the back of her neck.

Lachlan's intense, golden gaze was on Ty. "Why did she come to you?"

Ty pressed his tongue to his teeth. "Guess because I was a doctor."

Seth snorted. "You sure you have a genius IQ?"

Ty shot the man a bland look.

"We all saw the way you two were watching each other." Seth threw out a hand. "I'm surprised there wasn't smoke from the heat you two were generating."

"Enough." Lachlan swiveled. "Let's get to the Bunker."

They took Lachlan's SUV, and soon, Ty was walking back into the Bunker. The sun was just rising as he flicked on the lights inside. Seth went to work on the coffeemaker.

Lachlan dropped into Kinsey's chair and tapped on the computer. "Brooks, rise and shine."

A second later, Brooks appeared on screen, hair mussed and sliding his glasses on. "Man, don't you guys ever sleep?" He scraped a hand through his hair. "I was catching a few Zs while my search programs were running."

"Ty had another run-in with our friend," Lachlan said.

Brooks swiveled to look at Ty. "You bleeding? Anything broken?"

"She tied him to his bed," Seth shouted from the kitchenette.

Ty growled. "How about we focus? Brooks, did you find anything?"

Brooks was barely suppressing his laughter. "I used the name River, and our MI6 suspicion...and I tracked her down."

Ty's pulse jumped and he leaned forward.

"Her name is River Elliott-Hall."

River Elliott-Hall. Ty rolled the name around in his mouth.

"There's not much info on her. She worked for MI6 for several years, and all that's classified. Now, she's gone freelance. She's known for finding things and people, and returning them. She's good. She's got a good word-of-mouth reputation, and a one-hundred-percent success rate."

Lachlan grunted.

"She's also the daughter of an earl. Illegitimate."

Ty's head jerked up. "Who?"

"Henry Edward Hall, the Earl of Lindford. He had an affair with River's mother—Celeste Elliott. She was a British-Jamaican woman who worked in the earl's office for a while. During River's childhood, the good earl had River to his home to spend time with his family. He has two older sons."

Ty put a hand on his hip. He bet that was hell for her. This was the chip that was lodged deep in her shoulder.

"Seems she was close to the mother, who raised her," Brooks continued. "But Celeste Elliott died a few years back. Cancer."

So, for all intents and purposes, River was alone. Ty glanced out one of the small windows. The morning sun was lighting up all the airport's tarmacs. He knew all about being alone, even when you had a mother or father in the picture.

"From what I've been able to find, a mission went bad and an agent died. That's when she left MI6."

"Anything else?" Lachlan asked.

"I've also been running some discreet searches on the *Salvator Mundi*." Brooks sat back in his chair. "There are whispers that it's been stolen."

"River confirmed that," Ty said.

"What the hell is so special about this painting?" Lachlan demanded.

"I might have an answer." Brooks swiped his tablet.

Ty watched an image of the painting flash up. Seth appeared and handed him a mug of coffee.

"There appears to be some speculation about the orb that Jesus is holding," Brooks said.

Peering closer, Ty frowned. He took in the orb carefully. He could see straight through to Jesus' robes. "It isn't refracting the light."

"Ding-ding," Brooks said. "Da Vinci didn't paint any refraction of the light that would have been hitting the globe. It's been noted by experts, mainly because da Vinci was no slouch when it came to understanding optics. He'd done plenty of experiments, other paintings, and made plenty of notes about how light behaves."

"He did this deliberately," Lachlan said.

"What are the three bright spots on the sphere?" Seth asked.

Brooks lifted a shoulder. "No one knows."

"Keep digging," Lachlan ordered.

Ty stared at the image of the *Salvator Mundi*, his gaze zeroing in on the orb. *What the hell are you and what are you hiding?*

"So, where's Elliott-Hall now?" Lachlan looked at Ty.

Ty grabbed a tablet off Kinsey's desk and logged in with his fingerprint. He tapped into the secure Team 52 server, and pulled up his tracking program. It was highly unlikely that she would have discovered the small, flesh-colored tracker patch he'd pressed to her neck.

A map of Las Vegas filled the screen. "Looks like she's in downtown Vegas. Near the Fremont Street Experience."

"I think Ms. Elliott-Hall needs to be our guest at Area 52," Lachlan said. "We can question her there, and convince her to work *with* us. It's more secure, so she can't escape from the base."

Ty raised a brow. "January did."

Seth grinned. "That's my girl."

Lachlan snorted. "We weren't prepared for January to make a run for it, because we didn't realize you were being an asshole at the time."

Seth's smile faded.

"You think kidnapping River isn't asshole-ish behavior?" Ty asked.

"We'll beef up security," Lachlan said. "And then work to make sure River doesn't feel the need to run."

"She's concerned we'll take over and confiscate her find," Ty said.

Lachlan frowned. "Well, that will probably happen, but there is something more involved with this painting, and I don't want to be finding out what it is because people are dying." The Team 52 leader looked at the screen. "Brooks, call the rest of the team in."

"On it."

Ty was working through his second cup of coffee when the rest of Team 52 arrived.

Axel made a beeline for the coffeepot. Callie stood beside Blair, gaze watchful. Smith leaned against the wall.

"Busy night?" Blair asked silkily.

Ty swiveled in his chair. "Something like that." She sounded pissed that she'd missed out on the action.

"We're heading to Freemont Street," Lachlan said. "So, get prepped."

"For what?" Blair asked.

"We're going to bring in former MI6 agent, River Elliott-Hall."

Smith straightened. "Former MI6?"

"Yep," Seth said cheerfully. "And last night, she tied up Ty."

Blair swiveled. "I thought you handcuffed her?"

"This was after," Seth added helpfully. "She tied him to his bed."

"Kinky," Axel said.

Ty felt the weight of everyone's gazes. "Fuck, you guys are annoying."

"I suspect she isn't going to come with us easily," Callie said.

Lachlan nodded. "Pretty sure that's an understatement."

"Let me talk to her first," Ty said. "It could make it easier for all of us."

Lachlan stared at him. "Okay. But if she runs or attacks you, we're moving in. And no holding back."

Shit. Ty needed to convince her to come with them voluntarily. He nodded.

"Let's move," Lachlan said.

RIVER STROLLED down the Fremont Street covered pedestrian mall.

It was more of an experience at night, when the huge canopy roof covering the street was lit up. During the day, it looked a little less spectacular, and smelled vaguely of urine. She passed the Golden Nugget

Casino, remembering it was one of the oldest in the city.

It was such a gaudy contrast to the stately, plainer elegance of London's historic buildings, but she liked it. She liked the fact that Las Vegas gave the world the finger and shined brightly.

Despite it being early morning, there was still a reasonable crowd of pedestrians in the mall—tourists, shoppers, and some glassy-eyed gamblers who'd clearly been up all night in the casinos, imbibing the free drinks.

She'd retrieved her things from her crappy hotel and gotten changed out of Ty's too-large clothes. Her wound was starting to hurt a bit, as unfortunately, the drugs that Ty had given her were wearing off. She placed a stop at a pharmacy on her To Do list.

She pulled her denim jacket more tightly around her. She felt weary and she wished she was still snuggled up in Ty's bed, preferably with his warm body against hers.

The thought jolted River. She shook her head. She *never* slept with anybody. That was crazy.

"River."

She froze, looking up. Like her thoughts had summoned him, the crowd parted and she saw Ty walking toward her.

How the hell had he found her?

"We just want to help," he said.

We? She scanned her surroundings. Lachlan Hunter was standing near a souvenir shop, hands loose by his sides. The handsome Axel was near a group of tourists, big Smith was partly hidden by an enterprising busker dressed like the Statue of Liberty. She didn't spot the others, but she guessed that the rest of Team 52 was close by.

"How did you find me?"

He stayed silent.

She cursed. "You put a tracker on me."

"Let us help you."

Her jaw tightened. "I told you, I don't need help."

"The wound on your side says otherwise."

"It's fine."

"I can tell it's hurting you. Lean a little and let me help."

"You want to save me, Ty? Do I look helpless?"

"No, but I think you're lonely."

His words were like an arrow to her heart. No, a nasty little bug trying to worm under her skin.

"Well, I'm not." She turned around.

She sensed Ty lunge for her. He grabbed a fistful of her jacket and she twisted, letting the denim slide off her arms.

She sprinted into the crowd, dodging shoppers and tourists. Her side twinged, but she ignored it.

Suddenly, arms closed around her from behind, lifting her off her feet.

She turned her head and saw Axel's good-looking face. "Hey, there."

He scowled at her.

"Help!" River cried. "Help, my ex won't leave me alone. He's going to hurt me!"

Axel growled. "Quiet—"

"Hey." Two big bikers, both with bushy beards and

black-leather jackets, stepped in front of them. One grabbed Axel by the back of the neck.

As Axel was yanked away, he cursed, his hold on River loosening.

She heard the scuffle of a fight, but she didn't look back as she jogged away. She shouldered through a group of laughing women.

As she walked past a small crowd clustered around two buskers dressed in feathered showgirl outfits, River snatched a baseball cap off someone's head. Ducking, she slipped it over her head, tucking her curls back.

Shoulders hunched, she kept her gaze down and powered down the mall. Then she saw a pair of dark boots step into view.

She looked up and saw Seth.

"How about we do this the easy way, MI6?" he suggested.

"I've never been a fan of easy, CIA."

"Must be why you like Ty," Seth said.

River attacked. She got in a good chop to his side, but he was already swinging to block her next blow. She lifted her leg and kicked him. But the man was well-trained and knew how to fight. As they circled each other, his arm shot out. She ducked the punch.

He was good.

But she was better because he was trying not to hurt her.

River ducked, then rammed her head up. The top of her head caught him under the chin. She heard his pained grunt.

She shoved him hard, and he fell back into a woman

pushing a stroller. The mother screamed.

Seth tried to right himself, but River jumped up, and landed a hard kick to his chest. He fell back, sprawling on the ground.

She turned and ran.

She darted through the groups of people. Another block, and she'd be out of the mall and close to her rental car.

But she hadn't gone far when Smith stepped into her path.

River skidded to a halt and tried to dodge around the muscular man. He sidestepped, watching her steadily. Something about him made her feel like she was being hunted.

She edged closer to where she saw two teenage girls giggling together. Smith started toward her and River quickly grabbed one teen and shoved the girl at Smith.

The teenager crashed into him, her high-pitched screams echoing around them. Smith righted the girl, but one look at him, and the girl screamed louder. Her friend started screaming too.

River turned and powerwalked away.

But a second later, Lachlan and Blair appeared, standing shoulder to shoulder.

Damn, these guys were tenacious. River's side was throbbing now.

Blair walked forward. "I've been looking forward to this."

They launched at each other. River's focus narrowed down to the fight. She kicked and Blair blocked. They circled, and Blair came at River with a punch. River ducked, then rammed her own fist into Blair's gut. The woman barely reacted and grabbed at River's hair. She knocked River's stolen cap off and grabbed a handful of hair.

They turned in an untidy circle and River swiped at the woman.

Sensing movement behind her, River looked back and saw Lachlan moving closer. She kicked backward and jammed her foot into his gut. She yanked on Blair, and Blair yanked back. They broke apart.

A shocked crowd had circled around them, watching with excited, alarmed murmurs.

Lachlan came at River again. She spun and lunged into him. Grabbing his collar, she hooked a leg around his knee and shoved.

With a curse, he went down. Blair launched herself at River and River ducked. As Blair got close, River grabbed her shirt, and used the woman's momentum to toss her over River's shoulder. Blair landed flat on her back.

River jumped up and ran. She felt the blood seeping down her side. Dammit, she'd torn the cut open. She rushed into a nearby café.

She heard startled cries and looked back to see Blair charging at her. River grabbed a chair and threw it at the woman.

Then she turned and leaped onto a table. Plates smashed and people cried out. River jumped to the next table, then the next.

She kept running, and suddenly heard a whistle of air. She turned, and saw a red-tipped dart embed in the wall behind her. She shifted her gaze to a large mirror, and in it, she saw the reflection of Callie, who was holding a tranquilizer rifle. The dark-haired woman swiveled, aiming at River.

Fuck.

As Callie fired again, River was already leaping off the table.

She hit the ground and took off running. But a second later, she felt a sharp sting as a dart hit her in the back.

Damn. She reached over her shoulder and yanked it out.

She leaped through the panicked crowd and staggered out of the café. She rushed past the next store, knocking over racks of clothes and souvenirs.

"Hey!" someone shouted.

People screamed.

Keep moving, River. Her mouth was dry and her limbs were growing heavy.

She lurched across the mall. Everything around her was a blur of noise and color. Her feet felt too heavy to lift.

River tripped.

She was falling, the pavement rushing up to meet her. She didn't even have the strength to throw out her arms and break her fall.

But she didn't hit the ground.

Strong arms caught her, and she looked up into Ty's hard, handsome face.

"I've got you, River."

"Ty—"

And that's when River passed out.

CHAPTER SEVEN

Ty led the handcuffed and blindfolded River out of the elevator, and into the Area 52 base.

When Lachlan nodded, Ty reached up and untied the blindfold.

River's light-brown gaze clashed with his. She did not look happy. Then she looked past him, taking in the underground base.

Everything was matte-black metal with a dark floor. To the left were huge, floor-to-ceiling doors leading into the storage warehouse. River's eyes widened slightly. The doors were open at the moment, meaning Arlo—the crusty, former-military man who was the custodian of the warehouse—was in there somewhere. Rows and rows of shelves, all stacked with black, reinforced boxes, filled the space.

Then River looked to the right, taking in the glass-walled offices and the large rec room that made up the main work area for the team. Ahead of them, the rest of the team moved down the corridor. Blair shot one glare at River, which River returned with a very cool, British version.

Ty reached around behind her and undid her handcuffs. "I need to check your wound."

She shrugged, like she didn't care.

Lachlan still stood nearby, his arms crossed over his chest. "We'll meet in the comp lab when you've finished checking her over."

Ty nodded and waved a hand for River to precede him down the corridor.

They walked in silence past several offices. She made no effort to hide that she was memorizing every detail.

A door slammed open and an older man—with a stocky body clad in black fatigues and his gray hair cut military short—stomped toward them. River's steps slowed, and she eyed the man warily.

"Sampson." The man's voice was deep and gravelly.

"Arlo."

The man's faded blue eyes moved to River, narrowing in his grizzled face. "You the woman who's been hassling our team?"

She lifted her chin. "Yes. Who are you?"

"Name's Arlo Green."

"Arlo takes care of the storage facility," Ty said.

He watched as Arlo and River started a stare off. Ty tried to hide his amusement.

"You must do a decent job," River said.

"And you must be good to get the drop on my guys." Arlo grunted. "Heard you were with MI6?"

She nodded.

"Had an old buddy there, Royston Pike."

River's eyes widened. "Pike's a bit of a legend."

"Crusty old bugger."

Ty pressed his tongue to his teeth. Arlo calling anyone crusty was a classic pot and kettle situation.

River smiled. "I couldn't agree more."

Arlo gave a decisive nod. "Don't cause any trouble in my base while you're here."

"I don't make promises I can't keep."

The older man gave a grunt. "And don't drug or tie up my team again, either."

She shrugged a shoulder. "They let that happen, then they deserve it."

Arlo barked out a laugh. "I think I like you." Without another word, he stomped off down the corridor.

Ty raised a brow and nudged her forward. "I'm impressed, Arlo doesn't like anyone."

"So a kindred spirit for you, then?"

He ignored her and shouldered open the door to his lab.

Her eyebrows rose and she looked around with interest. "Your inner sanctum."

"Don't touch anything," he warned.

The faintest smile touched her lips. "You're as grumpy as Arlo."

"I haven't got time to be nice."

He pushed a stool out from a bench and she sat down, hitching her long legs around it. As she studied his benches—all loaded with various experiments and tests—he pulled out his medical kit. He set it out on a trolley and wheeled it over.

"Shirt up."

She cocked her head. "I usually like a little more fore-play before I get my clothes off."

"River," he said with exaggerated patience.

She lifted the hem of her shirt. He removed the blood-soaked bandage and checked her wound. She stayed very still.

There was all that shiny, smooth skin. It was shades lighter than his own. He dragged his mind off her skin and onto stopping the sluggish bleeding. "At least you didn't tear your stitches out."

"So, we're next door to the infamous Area 51?"

He opened some antiseptic and dabbed it onto a cloth. He cleaned the injury. "That's classified."

As he stroked her skin, she shivered.

Ty reached over and grabbed a fresh bandage. He gently pressed it over the cut. "There. If I had any lollipops, I'd give you one."

As their gazes met, he felt the hot arc of connection. It was like a thread he could almost touch. He moved his fingers and stroked the warm skin of her belly.

Her eyelids fluttered, then her lips firmed. "I hate how much you make me feel."

"I know," he said. "I feel the same way. It's far easier not to feel, not to care."

"Those mommy and daddy issues again?"

He shrugged. "My parents are workaholics. I was just something to check off their list. The only emotions they display towards me are intense displeasure and disappointment that I'm not working at my father's company, making billions of dollars." He kept his tone matter-of-fact.

She released a breath. "You're right. It would be smarter for us to ignore this...attraction."

Ty fought a smile. "I like how you say attraction the same way you'd say insanity."

"It is crazy."

He stood, shifting between her legs. She reached up and gripped his shoulders.

Then he lowered his head, slowly, giving her time to pull back if she wanted. But she didn't move. In fact, she closed the last inch between their lips.

He felt her sigh against his lips before he kissed her. He took his time tasting her, opening her lips, his tongue touching hers.

She tasted too damn good, and he felt like a starving man.

But even as he tried to keep it slow and easy, hunger ignited in his gut. He tilted her head back and deepened the kiss, sliding his tongue across hers. Her hands gripped him tighter, pulling him closer. She matched him, her tongue thrusting back against his.

They both groaned.

Then the lab door opened.

"Oops. Sorry, I wasn't here." Nat beat a hasty retreat out of the lab.

Ty sighed, pressing his forehead to River's. "Everyone busts in here whenever it suits them."

"Poor baby."

"Come on." He straightened. "We need to get to the comp lab."

She slid off the stool and he pressed a hand to her lower back. He felt the faint tremor in her body.

She sucked in a breath. "Yep, I don't like what you do to me."

"Too bad."

As he led her into the comp lab, Brooks was standing in the center of the room. The younger man looked up, his eyes widening behind his glasses as he took them in. He studied River with unabashed interest.

"So, you're our former MI6 intruder," Brooks said.

"Hey there, hunky," River said.

Brooks smiled at her.

"I like your shirt," she said.

"Clearly you have good taste."

Today, Brooks' T-shirt had an Imperial walker from Star Wars drinking out of a toilet on the front of it. Ty grunted and scowled at Brooks.

The younger man straightened. "I'm Brooks, guru of all things electronic."

River nodded. "The computer geek."

Brooks shrugged one muscular shoulder. He was comfortable with his skills, and despite the big brain and glasses, Ty knew he was no slouch in a fight. Still, he could do without the man flirting with River.

The doors opened behind them and when Ty looked over, he watched the director of Team 52 enter. Somehow, whenever Jonah Grayson entered a room, he owned it.

He wore a dark suit and a white shirt that was bright against his bronze skin. His black hair was neatly styled, and his sharply handsome face was dominated by high cheekbones and bright-green eyes.

River stiffened. Ty reached out and touched the small of her back.

Jonah's piercing green gaze fell on River. "I'm Director Jonah Grayson."

"The boss man," River said.

Jonah gave her a faint smile. "Yes." Then his face hardened. "Ms. Elliott-Hall, my team are going to find the *Salvator Mundi*. We'd prefer to work with you to achieve that."

"My other option being?" River asked sardonically.

"Rather than us taking you out of the equation and locking you up."

She sniffed. "Fair enough. I guess I'll go with option one."

"No more breaking and entering into Team 52 premises, or drugging my people." Jonah's voice held a dark edge. "Or tying them up." He glanced at Ty.

Great. Lachlan had obviously reported in. The team would continue to have a field day ribbing him.

"Your team has drugged and tied me up as well," River said.

"Then everyone is even," Jonah said. "Now, let's work together and find the painting."

Lachlan shifted his big body. "You start by talking."

River let her gaze move around the room, and Ty felt compelled to keep his fingers at the small of her back. He knew she hardly needed the support, but she didn't pull away. She dragged in a deep breath. "The *Salvator Mundi* was stolen from the Louvre Abu Dhabi."

"You're sure?" Jonah asked.

"Yes. A four-man team snuck in. The museum is located on an island, and is surrounded by water. The thieves SCUBA-dived in, and entered through some drainage pipes."

"Then?" Lachlan prompted.

"Then I was hired. As you deduced, I'm former MI6, but I freelance now."

"You have a good reputation," Jonah said. "And you're expensive."

"Because I'm good. I conducted my investigation, and discovered a private jet left Abu Dhabi a few hours after the theft. Eyewitness reports say that a secret parcel was snuck aboard the aircraft just before it took off."

"And it came to Las Vegas?" Ty asked.

She nodded, her curls bobbing. "The jet belonged to Chadwick Alton."

Jonah frowned. "The casino owner?"

She nodded again.

"Man owns half of Vegas." Lachlan looked at Brooks. "Pull what we have on Alton."

Brooks swiped at his tablet. "He's seventy years old. Owns or part-owns a bunch of casinos and hotels. He's in real estate, too...actually, he dabbles in a lot of stuff. Retail, pharmaceuticals, manufacturing." Brooks looked up. "He's also an avid art collector."

"I searched the private art gallery he keeps at his newest casino—the Constellation," River said. "The *Salvator Mundi* wasn't there." She pointed to her side, lifting her shirt to show the bandage. "He caught a glimpse of me on a security camera. He wasn't happy about the intrusion."

"Did he identify you?" Ty asked.

She shook her head. "I don't think so. I wouldn't be in their database, and his thugs didn't use my name."

"They probably just used security cameras to match your face and find where you were," Brooks said. "Easy enough for a decent tech guy to do."

"So, if Alton has the painting," Blair said, "where is it?"

"It'll be at his mansion," River said.

Pictures of the mansion appeared on the screen.

Axel let out a whistle. "Looks like a replica of the White House."

The large house was very white, with lots of columns. The lawns around it were lush and green, so Ty guessed Alton had a hell of a water bill.

"It's out in Summerlin," Brooks added. "Backs onto a golf course, and the street is chock full of giant houses. Some people call it Billionaire's Row, although a few streets duke it out for that moniker now."

Lachlan studied the images, then nodded. "Let's plan a little visit."

River turned. "It would be better if I go in alone—"

Ty shifted closer. "No. You aren't alone anymore."

"And this isn't our first rodeo, River," Lachlan said. "We're perfectly capable of getting in and out without being seen."

River let out a breath. "Fine."

"HERE YOU GO. MY FAVORITE TEA."

River accepted the cup and saucer from Natalie. "Thanks."

She stood in the swanky rec room with Nat, Blair, and Callie. River wasn't entirely sure if the women were feeling her out, or planning to murder her and hide the body.

They'd, not very subtly, shuffled her out of the comp room where the team was planning the upcoming mission to Alton's mansion. River watched them, waiting for whatever the hell they wanted to come out.

The team's archeologist was dressed like she was about to hit a boardroom or a library. Her skirt and shirt contrasted sharply with the black cargo pants and T-shirts of the other women.

Nearby, Blair was watching River like a hawk. Callie was sitting, drinking a soda. She was a bit more welcoming, but the coiled tension in the woman's athletic body said she could easily explode into action if required.

River sipped the tea. *Mmm.* She loved a good cup of tea.

"So, I saw you and Ty sharing a super-sexy kiss." Nat fanned her face. "So hot."

Ahh, there was the shot across the bow.

Blair stiffened. "What?"

"Really?" Callie drawled, a grin on her lips. "I'm impressed. You got past all the dark, brooding spikes he's covered in?"

River shrugged a shoulder. "He's hot, and he helped me."

"So, that's it?" Blair snapped. "He's hot, so you thought you'd stick your tongue down his throat?"

"He kissed me." River sipped her tea again. "Don't worry, Mason, I don't do long-term. So, you don't have to worry that I'll suck your friend into my evil web."

Blair grunted, clearly unconvinced.

"Knives in, Mason," Callie murmured.

River set down her cup. "Look, you brought me in here, when I'd much prefer to be back in the comp room going over the mission plan—"

Callie waved a hand. "The mission is planned. The guys just like to go over it to death, looking all alpha-male and menacing."

"I've agreed to work with you guys," River continued. "All I want is to find the *Salvator Mundi*. Once this mission is done, I'll be on the first plane back to London."

Blair stared at her for a long moment, then nodded. "Fine."

River nodded.

Then Blair pointed. "But if you do anything to risk my team, I'm coming for you."

Ty wasn't the only prickly person around here.

"And if you hurt Ty in any way, you're a dead woman," Blair drawled.

Nat made a squeaking sound.

River tilted her head. "You think you can take me, Mason?"

Blair smiled, tossing her blonde ponytail over her shoulder. "Oh, yeah, MI6."

"I have no intention of hurting Ty." The words

rushed out of River and she bit her lip. Dammit, she'd do what she had to in order to get her job done.

As she looked up, Blair was watching her, something working through her mis-matched eyes. Callie had a faint smile on her face, and Nat was trying to hide her grin behind her cup.

"Is this interrogation over?" River asked.

"I think so," Nat said.

"Good."

River happily headed back to the computer room. The men were all standing around the central table, going over the infiltration plan.

Wow. As River studied the screens, she saw schematics and aerial photos of Alton's mansion. These guys had access to good intel. She also saw a picture of Alton, himself.

She ground her teeth together. Grief and anger flooded her before she locked them down. This man was the reason Jack had died. Alton had been at the warehouse that day for an arms deal, and because of his shady dealings, Jack had paid the price.

She'd never been able to prove it. She sucked in a breath. Her superiors at MI6 had told her to drop it, which was a big reason she'd left. But none of her own investigations had ever linked Alton to that deal.

Blowing out a breath, she focused on the screens again. For now, the painting was her priority, not the past. She kept telling herself that this wasn't personal. It was just a job.

But it was hard to turn off the anger every time she saw the bastard's face. And she'd be lying if, once she'd known Alton was involved with the *Salvator Mundi*, it hadn't sparked a need to put the asshole in his place.

The jumpy feeling in her gut told her otherwise.

Seth tapped a finger to the map. "We should infiltrate here."

"We'll split into three teams," Lachlan said. "The painting is either in his office, the bedroom vault, or in his art gallery."

There were nods all around.

"I'm coming," Ty said.

Lachlan lifted his head and frowned at him.

"You know I can do it," Ty said.

"You have work here—" Lachlan started.

"I'm coming." Ty's voice was firm as stone.

Blair was staring at Ty. "He is required to do a couple missions in the field every year to keep his rating up. It's been a while."

Lachlan released a long breath, his gaze flicking to River, then back again. "Fine."

"We need to get River some armor and gear," Blair said.

River smiled. The woman sounded like she'd prefer to do anything else than include River on this mission.

"I'll do it," Ty said.

Lachlan nodded. "We'll go in tonight. Now—" he pinned his stare on River "—it's time for you to share what is so special about the *Salvator Mundi*."

Damn, she should have known they wouldn't give up. "It's worth four hundred and fifty million dollars," River answered. "Isn't that enough?"

"I think we all know it's more than that," Ty said.

"You thought we had it, and we don't deal in pricey artifacts unless they possess something...more."

She looked at them all for a moment. She'd agreed to work with these people. "There's a map hidden in the picture."

Ty nodded. "Classic Leonardo da Vinci. It's the orb, isn't it?"

Of course, Ty had worked it out. She nodded. "It leads to a da Vinci device."

"Hell," Axel muttered.

"That's why Alton stole the painting?" Ty said.

"Likely."

"Couldn't you decode the map from a photo of the painting?" Callie asked.

River shook her head. "The painting has had extensive restoration done on it. Old layers of paint have been removed since photographs have been taken of it."

"And photos can be unreliable," Ty added. "The dimensions and colors distorted."

"Why does Alton want the orb?" Lachlan asked.

"He's a fanatic, driven by greed," River said. "Like Brooks said, he's got fingers in lots of pies. What Brooks didn't uncover is that Alton is a narcissist, and he believes in transhumanism."

"Really?" Brooks pulled a face.

"Which is what?" Lachlan asked.

Ty shifted. "The belief in using technology to enhance the human body and intellect. To transform us into something better, more advanced."

"Fuck," Blair muttered.

River nodded. "Lots of transhumanists believe in

advancement for all, but Alton has special interest in eugenics, and a lack of interest in ethics getting in his way."

"Eugenics, like a master race?" Lachlan asked. "Like Hitler and his Aryan race?"

"Something like that," River said. "Except Alton doesn't believe in the Aryan race, he believes that he has to create this special group of people. He wants to be in charge of selecting the special few."

Smith grunted. "I hate assholes."

Ty had gone still. His gaze narrowed on her. "You've crossed paths with Alton before."

Damn him for being so perceptive. "Unfortunately, yes." She lifted her chin. "While I was with MI6. He was responsible for the death of my partner."

Silence filled the room.

"This is personal for you," Ty said.

River straightened. "I don't do personal. This is just a job."

Lachlan rubbed the bridge of his nose. "It's always personal."

"Alton was in London for an arms deal at the warehouse where my partner was killed." Even now, she remembered running down that alley, her boots pounding on the pavement. *Late. Too late.* "I can't prove he ordered the kill, but he was there, and he's dirty."

"Arms?" Blair's lip curled.

River nodded. "One of Alton's hidden side businesses."

"Stellar guy," Seth muttered.

Nat cleared her throat. "I'm sorry about your partner, River."

She felt them watching her. Felt Ty's gaze trying to peer inside her head. "Thanks."

"The device the painting leads to?" Nat asked. "Do you know what it is?"

Focusing on the painting helped her control the old emotions swirling in her belly. "It's the orb itself."

Nat's face lit up. "Really?"

"What does it do?" Ty asked.

River shrugged. "No one knows. But if it was made by da Vinci, I'm guessing it does something amazing."

"I'll pull the *Arno* and the *Angelica*." Nat spun and left the room, her heels clicking on the floor.

"The *Arno* and the *Angelica*?" River asked.

"We have two of da Vinci's notebooks in our storage facility," Lachlan said. "The Codex *Arno* and the Codex *Angelica*."

River's mouth dropped open. "Seriously?"

"Seriously. Now, let's go over our plan to get into Alton's mansion again."

CHAPTER EIGHT

"All set?" Ty asked.

He watched River check over the SIG Sauer handgun before she slid it into the holster on her hip. She was all decked-out in black, tactical gear like he was.

"I'd forgotten how great it is to have unlimited resources," she said.

"Just call me Q." He held out his palm, a tiny earpiece resting on it.

She fitted the small device in her ear.

Ty pulled back. "So, you had a partner?"

She stiffened and he saw the shutters come down. Damn, he never thought he'd meet someone more closed up than himself.

"His name was Jack. He was ten years older than me, like an older brother. He trained me."

"You were close."

"Yes." She glanced away. "Now he's dead."

"You blame yourself," Ty said quietly.

Turbulent eyes met his. "Can we not talk about this?"

Strangely, Ty wanted her to talk to him, to hear her secrets. "Okay." He wouldn't push her. Not now.

He handed over the high-tech, experimental CXM7 assault rifle he'd developed for Team 52. "Probably won't need this, but we'll bring it, just in case."

She took it reverently. "Wow, now, this is one hell of a weapon." Her fingers slid over the smooth metal.

"It's my design." He pointed. "It has an integrated grenade launcher and a combat shotgun, as well as assisted targeting."

"You're kidding." Her gaze met his. "It makes me want to kiss you."

He felt his gut tighten. "I won't stop you."

She stared into his eyes. "This is a bad idea."

"Undoubtedly." He dropped a quick kiss to her lips, not rushing, drawing in the taste of her.

For a second, she leaned into him.

Then she straightened. "You sure you should come on this mission?"

"I can hold my own, River."

She eyed him up and down. "I believe it." She was silent for a minute. "Ty?"

"Yeah?"

She slung the rifle over her shoulder, then reached up, pressing her hands to his chest. "After we find the *Salvator Mundi*, I want to fuck you."

Ty's cock went hard as steel in an instant.

River's lips curved. "I want to bang your brains out and get this out of our systems. Then I can get on the plane back to London in peace."

"A sensible plan." Damn, his voice held a husky edge. He let his hands slide down her body, cupping her ass. "We might need a few days."

Her mouth dropped open. "Days?"

"Oh, yeah. There's a lot involved in a proper banging."

She smiled slowly. "You're on, Sampson."

"Now, can you focus on the mission and not my bangability?"

She rolled her eyes. "I think I'll manage."

Together, they walked to the elevator, and were soon zooming upward. He led her into the hangar that sat above the underground base.

"Area 52 is more commonly known as Tonopah Test Range. It's a restricted military installation northwest of Area 51." He nodded at the Air Force guards standing nearby, cradling weapons. When he led her outside, and her gaze fell on the team's X8 jet-copter, she let out a gasp.

"Another of your designs?"

He nodded. "It combines the best characteristics of a helicopter and a plane. It has twin rotors on top, and jet engines on the modified wings."

When they climbed aboard the X8, the others were already seated. Blair and Seth, the team's pilots, were in the cockpit, running their preflight checks. Callie and Smith were checking over weapons in the back, and Lachlan and Axel were talking quietly.

Lachlan looked up and lifted his chin.

Ty settled into a seat and River sat down beside him.

Before long, they were flying over the desert, heading

toward Las Vegas. The sun was setting, turning the sands below a burnt gold.

"We don't get sunsets like this back home," River said. "Usually too many dull-gray clouds."

Then the lights of Las Vegas appeared, like a mirage in the growing darkness. Seth and Blair swooped them in to land like a helicopter. They touched down in front of the Bunker, the rotors slowing.

Kinsey jogged out to meet them. As soon as the team hit the tarmac, the blonde raced over to give Smith a quick kiss. The big man swept an arm around her, lifting her off her feet.

"I have the SUVs ready," Kinsey said a little breathlessly, her cheeks pink. "You need anything else, just let me know."

"Thanks, Kinsey," Lachlan said.

Kinsey smiled, although her eyes stayed serious. "Be careful."

They headed to the black SUVs out front. Ty held the door open for River, while the team packed boxes of weapons and gear in the back.

Then Seth slid behind the wheel, with Lachlan beside him in the passenger seat. River was wedged between Smith and Ty, while the rest of the team took the second vehicle.

They pulled out onto the road, the second vehicle following behind them. It was a quiet ride to Alton's mansion in Summerlin.

"What if he doesn't have it?" River muttered. "What if he has nothing to do with the painting?"

"One step at a time." Ty gripped her thigh and squeezed.

When he looked up, Lachlan was watching him with serious eyes. Ty sat back. Lachlan didn't miss a thing, ever.

They pulled off a few streets away from Alton's mansion, near the golf course. Brooks' voice came through the dash of the SUV.

"Feed incoming. Kinsey sent a drone up for me and I have thermal imaging for you. You'll see where Alton's guards are located. And I've confirmed Alton isn't in residence. He's at the Constellation."

Ty pulled out his tablet, studying the imagery Brooks had sent. It was an aerial shot of the huge house and several blotches of orange were moving around the grounds.

"Guards roaming the grounds," Ty said. "And at the main entrances."

Lachlan nodded and pushed open his door. Soon, the team came together, everyone checking their weapons again.

"We'll leave the CXMs," Lachlan said. "Handguns only. I'd prefer no one see us."

Everyone nodded.

"Let's move, 52," Lachlan ordered.

They fell into a tight group, filing onto the golf course. The grass was damp and he guessed it had just been watered. Ty walked right behind River. She moved with ease, silent and liquid. It was clear she was good at sneaking around. Soon, the large walls surrounding Alton's estate came into view.

Brooks' voice came through their earpieces. "Cameras are down, and the feed is on a loop. Alton's guards are looking at footage from twenty minutes ago."

"Acknowledged," Blair murmured.

They reached the wall and Smith knelt, holding his hands cupped together. Callie stood beside him, handgun in her hands, scanning around. They were the team's lookout and backup.

Lachlan put his boot in Smith's hands, and then boosted himself over the wall. Blair, Seth, and Axel followed. Then it was River's turn. With a boost from Smith, she sailed up and climbed easily over the stone wall.

Ty went last. He climbed over the fence and dropped down the other side in a crouch.

Lachlan gave them a hand signal and they broke off, heading toward the main house. There was a sprawling pool area, and some smaller buildings that were guest and staff quarters.

Lachlan and Seth broke off, heading to the left. Blair and Axel disappeared into the darkness like ghosts. River and Ty snuck through the manicured gardens. The house loomed ahead, gleaming white in the bright exterior lights.

They stayed crouched in some thick bushes and watched a guard saunter past. The man looked bored.

River lifted a hand and pointed. Ty studied the patio and the door that was their point of entry. The French doors were open. *Handy*. He nodded.

They rose and sprinted to the patio. They crossed the

marble tiles, hurried along the wall, and snuck in through the open doorway.

They stayed low, moving across a living area done in an overblown style with red velvet furniture and a lot of gold leaf. Ty winced. At least his parents had some style when they decorated. River pointed and they moved into a wide hallway.

"We're in the bedroom," Lachlan murmured. He was paired with Seth.

"Approaching the office," Blair said. She was with Axel.

Ty and River were headed to the art gallery.

Adrenaline pumped through Ty's veins. It had been a while since he'd been in the field. He kept his breathing steady and footsteps silent.

River stopped at a large set of wooden doors. They were carved with images of vines and cherubs. She tested the handle and shook her head. Locked.

She pulled out a lock pick, knelt, and set to work. Damn, he liked watching her work. Who knew he'd find her breaking and entering such a turn-on?

The door clicked open, and she shot him a smile. She had a beautiful smile that lit up her face. He gave her a nod. They slid inside and closed the door behind them.

Inside, the main gallery lights were dark, but there was a row of low lighting along the base of the walls. Ty scanned the large space. It was filled with amazing artwork.

As he took in the gilt frames and large sculptures, he didn't recognize anything famous. But art wasn't his thing, and knowing Alton, he was sure everything was by world-renowned artists and expensive as hell. Ty preferred to buy gadgets and devices for his lab, but each to their own.

They quickly moved through the windowless room, scanning all the artwork.

At the end, River straightened, and gave one frustrated shake of her head.

The *Salvator Mundi* wasn't here.

Shit. Ty hoped the others had better luck.

Suddenly, the sharp creak of an opening door echoed from the far end of the gallery.

They both spun.

"Guard," River murmured.

Ty frantically looked around. There weren't any places to hide.

He scanned the walls, and spotted the outline of a closet door. It was set into the wall and designed to look invisible. He grabbed River's wrist and yanked her toward it.

He pushed on the handleless door and it clicked open. Without even looking, he pulled her inside and closed the door behind them.

They stood in a tight space, pressed together in the pitch-black darkness.

THEY WERE in some sort of storage closet. Faint light seeped under the door, and as River's eyes adjusted, she spotted a few empty frames stacked against the wall.

Shelves at the back were filled with tools, dusters, and mops.

She heard footsteps echoing through the gallery and tensed.

She was pressed close to Ty, his big body surrounding hers, and she felt his breath on her cheek.

For a second, she was completely distracted, remembering exactly what he looked like without his shirt on. She shook her head. God, she'd never been so distracted in the middle of a mission before.

She *really* needed to get this man out of her system.

The footsteps paused and she imagined the guard turning in a circle. Then, the steps started heading back again.

"Thank God," she whispered.

They heard the click of the door closing. Ty moved, but she grabbed his wrist.

"Wait," she warned.

They stood there in the darkness for several more minutes. Then Ty carefully opened the closet door and peered out. He nodded, and they slid back out into the art gallery.

"We need to have another look around," Ty said. "Make sure the painting isn't here."

With a nod, they did another loop of the room.

"River," Ty whispered.

He was at the end of the gallery again. As she reached him, she realized he'd found another door set into the wall.

He pushed on it and the panel opened.

She expected to see another closet, but gasped. Inside was another room. As they entered, lights clicked on.

One wall was covered in bottles of what she guessed was expensive wine. In the center of the room, a round, glossy wooden table and leather chairs were set up. And on the other wall, were several paintings.

She guessed Alton liked to entertain his billionaire friends while surrounded by expensive wine and artwork. *Rich people.* She'd prefer Thai take-out on the couch while watching TV any day.

"River?"

Ty's voice jerked her out of her musings. That's when she saw that one painting on the wall was draped in dark-red silk.

Like it was waiting to be unveiled.

Heart pumping, she moved to it. She gripped the silk and whisked it off.

She gasped.

"The *Salvator Mundi,*" Ty murmured.

She grinned at Ty and he shot her a sexy smile.

Don't dissolve into a puddle of lust, River. She carefully checked the painting. She couldn't see any security system. She lifted it off the wall and checked the back. The painting was on wood, which was true for the *Salvator Mundi.* Da Vinci had most often painted on wood.

She nodded. "Let's go."

Ty pressed a finger to his ear. "Lachlan, we got it."

"What?" Lachlan said.

"We've got the *Salvator Mundi.*"

"Hell," Lachlan muttered.

Ty frowned. "What's wrong?"

"We got it, too."

River froze. *Fuck.* Alton was playing games. She checked the painting in her hands again. "This looks real, but I'm not an expert."

"Ours looks legit, too," Lachlan said. "Just bring it. We'll work it out later."

River nodded, and with Ty, headed back into the gallery. They moved right up the center of the room, circling around one large sculpture.

In the light, River noticed the glimmer of something close to the floor. Her brain was a second too slow to process what she was seeing.

She watched Ty step into the wire.

"What the fuck?" He stumbled, but righted himself.

"Tripwire!" she cried.

There was a rumble beneath their feet.

Boom.

The world exploded around them. River was lifted off her feet, the painting flying out of her hands.

She was tossed through the air and engulfed in noise and smoke. Then she slammed into the floor.

Groaning, she rolled onto her belly. She felt debris hit her back and winced.

"Ty!"

She looked around, coughing in the smoke. She spotted his body only meters away. He was on his side, rubble littering him.

"Ty!"

He didn't move. River coughed again. The smoke was getting thicker.

CHAPTER NINE

Ty shook his head. His temples were throbbing and his ears were ringing.

"Ty?"

He managed to look up, even though his head felt like a block of cement. River was crawling toward him. She was covered in dust, with a trickle of blood on her cheek.

"You okay?" He cupped the side of her head, checking her over. It was just a small cut.

She nodded. "Oh, God. Alton set a *bomb* in here." Then her eyes widened. "Your shoulder."

Ty looked down at the shard of metal embedded in his shoulder. *Shit.* He couldn't even feel it.

"Pull it out," he ordered. "It isn't deep enough to have penetrated anything vital."

Her mouth firmed into a hard line. She gripped the metal, then yanked fast.

Now he felt it. As pain speared through his upper body, he groaned.

"Ty? Ty?" Lachlan's tense voice in their earpieces.

As River pressed a wad of something against his bleeding wound, Ty touched his ear. "We're here. We're both alive."

"Thank fuck. What happened?"

"Bomb."

"Get out. We're aborting the mission."

With River's help, Ty managed to get to his feet. "Where's the *Salvator Mundi*?"

Both of them looked around.

"Shit." She nodded her head.

The painting was in the rubble. It was broken into shreds and ripped from the frame.

River knelt, touching the splintered wood. Then she fingered the ruined frame. "Look."

He glanced where she pointed. The wood near the edge was bright and new.

"It's a fake," she said.

"Good, now let's get out of here." Right now, Ty didn't give a flying fuck about the painting.

Together, they stumbled toward the door. Ty leaned against the wall as she grabbed the handle.

The door didn't budge. She jiggled it. "Locked."

"Where are your lock picks?"

She patted her pockets. "No idea." She looked back at the rubble.

Dammit. Biting back the pain from his shoulder, Ty kicked his boot against the door. The damn thing was sturdy and it didn't open.

"Step back." River lifted her handgun and fired at the lock.

Ty winced at the noise, then tried the door again. It still didn't move. "It must be barricaded from the other side."

"We're trapped in here," she said.

"Lachlan." Ty touched his earpiece. "The door to the gallery is barricaded. We're trapped in here."

"Acknowledged," Lachlan answered. "We'll get there as soon as we can. We've just engaged some of the guards."

Ty limped away from the door, scanning the room. "We need another way out."

"There are no windows."

He glanced at her. "You think Alton would design a space with only one entrance?"

She considered the smoky space. "You think there's another way out?"

He made a humming sound, and with River by his side, they headed back to the wine room.

Ty coughed. The smoke was growing thicker and flames were still flickering in the main gallery.

If they didn't find a way out soon, smoke inhalation would become a big risk. He circled the wine room, shoving some furniture out of the way.

He shoved a leather armchair aside and his blood ran cold.

"River."

She moved up beside and gasped. "Oh, fuck."

There was another bomb.

River knelt, studying the bomb's controls. "Why the fuck did he plan this?"

"Because he knew someone would come for the

painting. He wanted to stop them and send a message."

"Well, message received." Her shoulders sagged. "This device is bigger."

It was on a timer, no doubt triggered by the first explosion. Their eyes met. They had a little over two minutes left.

Ty spun. "Lachlan, get out."

"What?" Lachlan barked.

"There's a bigger bomb. Less than two minutes until it detonates."

Lachlan cursed. "We aren't leaving you guys."

"No time. Go, or we'll all be dead."

Ty heard a string of curses.

"Go." Ty's gaze locked with River's "We'll try and find a way out."

Her eyes were huge, her chest rising and falling fast. He pulled her toward him.

This time, she leaned into him, her hands gripping him hard. Ty took her mouth with his.

In that moment, there was no rubble or smoke or ticking time bomb. Just the two of them and the sensation of being in the right place.

River pulled her lips from his. "I'm not really keen to explode into a bloody death tonight."

"Okay. Then let's find a way out of here."

They moved along the walls of the wine room. Ty tested all the wine bottles, looking for any secret exits. River touched the paintings on the wall.

Something clicked.

Ty spun and saw a large painting swing away from the wall.

"Vault," River said. "Not a way out." She knocked a fist against the steel door. It had an old-fashioned dial lock. "It's thick. Think it could withstand a bomb blast?"

"I think the more important question is can you open it in—" he glanced at the bomb "—one and a half minutes?"

She smiled. "Watch me."

She dropped down in front of the door and pressed her ear to the lock. Ty was very conscious of the fact that she had no tools, no tech, no fancy devices. Just skills and determination.

Ty tried to block out the ticking bomb across the room. He drew in a deep breath. This wasn't how he'd choose to go, but some part of him was glad that he was with River.

"Lachlan, we found a vault. River's trying to get us inside." He watched her gently turning the dial one way, then the next.

He was well aware that the likelihood that she could break into the vault was low. Shit, he hated feeling helpless.

Click. She looked back over her shoulder and spun the vault door handle. Several dark spirals of hair fell over her eyes and she grinned. "Got it."

Ty grabbed her arm and pushed her inside the vault. He slammed the door closed behind them.

Inside, bright-blue security lights lit the space. It was packed with more artwork, and several stacks of gold bars.

"Yowser." River took it all in. "How much do you think all this is worth?"

Ty didn't even look. Glancing at his watch, he slid an arm around River. "It's time."

Her hands gripped him.

Boom.

The ground beneath them rocked, and they wrapped their arms around each other. Something fell off a shelf.

Then everything was quiet. They were breathing and unharmed.

They grinned at each other. Sensation flooded Ty like a tidal wave. They were alive. He yanked her up on her toes and kissed her.

She made a hungry humming sound and threw her arms around his neck. *More.* He needed more. He devoured her. Desire was like a supernova, fueled by the extreme circumstances. She moaned and wrapped herself around him.

Her momentum knocked him back against a shelf and he gripped her harder. He needed more than just the sweet, tart taste of her mouth. He wanted her surrender. He wanted to watch this fascinating woman come apart for him.

Suddenly, his hands dropped and he tore at her trousers.

"*Yes.* Ty." Her eyes were glazed, her voice husky. "Hurry."

She reached down to help. Finally, he had the fastening free and he violently shoved her trousers and panties down her thighs. Then he slid his hand between her legs and stroked.

"Oh." She made a shocked, choked cry.

This was what he wanted. Her pleasure. He pumped two fingers inside her.

River cried out, her thighs clamping around his wrist. He plunged his fingers in, again and again. He moved his thumb to stroke her clit.

She moaned. "I'm...fuck."

River broke apart, coming with a sharp cry.

Ty stilled, his body a throbbing mass of need. Her head dropped against his shoulder, and the space filled with their harsh pants.

"That was..." She let out a gusty breath. Then her hand slid down and cupped his rock-hard cock through his trousers. "Awesome."

Ty groaned.

Suddenly, there was a knock on the vault door. "Ty? River?"

Lachlan.

They both froze. River let out a choked laugh.

Ty cleared his throat. "We're okay."

"Me more than anybody else," River murmured under her breath.

He helped her pull her panties and trousers back up, then they both turned...and went still.

"Holy hell," River muttered.

The *Salvator Mundi* was resting against the far wall.

And this time, Ty had no doubt it was the real thing. It seemed to emanate with a special feel Ty couldn't quite describe. He was a man of science, but even he sensed something special. The gaze of the man in the picture was otherworldly, and the orb in his palm seemed to glow.

RIVER LET Ty help her over the wall.

She was sore and bleeding from several scratches. Callie had already done some quick first-aid on her, and on Ty's shoulder. She glanced at him. If he was in any pain, she couldn't tell.

Biting her lip, she watched Seth and Axel handling the painting carefully as they moved over the wall of Alton's estate.

Maybe working with others wasn't so bad.

In the distance, she heard sirens.

"Let's move a bit faster," Lachlan ordered.

Team 52 hurried back to the SUVs. Seth and Axel slid the painting into a large, reinforced black box in the back of the vehicle.

"Blair, update MacKade on what happened," Lachlan said.

Blair made a sound. "Oh, he's going to love this."

Everyone slid into the vehicles. As soon as the doors were closed, the two SUVs pulled out, driving slowly. River knew they wouldn't want to draw any attention to themselves. The SUV in front of them veered off in a different direction as they split up.

River leaned her head back against the seat. Ty was a big, solid warmth beside her. He slid an arm along the seat behind her.

"What I can't figure out is, why leave the painting?" Seth said from the driver's seat. "Why risk letting a bomb destroy it?"

Ty scowled. "Because Alton is crazy?"

Lachlan stared straight ahead. "Or maybe he didn't need it anymore."

River stiffened. "You think he already decoded the orb map off it?"

"Maybe."

Quiet fell in the SUV.

"We can speculate more in the morning," Lachlan said. "We'll drop everyone off to shower and rest up. We'll regroup at the Bunker in the morning." Lachlan looked at Ty. "Get that shoulder sorted out."

"It's fine. I have what I need back at my place to treat it."

"I want the *Salvator Mundi* with me," River said.

Lachlan's gaze narrowed like a laser beam.

She held up a palm. "I'm not going to run off with it. I promise."

"River's with me," Ty said.

She looked sideways at him. His strong features were in shadow.

"River?" Lachlan asked.

She nodded. For the first time in a long time, she just switched off and let someone else take care of things. Before she realized what she was doing, she let her head drop against Ty's uninjured shoulder.

"I have the best security to ensure the safety of the painting." Ty's amused gaze flicked to River. "Especially since I've had reason to upgrade my system recently."

Satisfied, Lachlan nodded and turned back in his seat.

When Seth pulled up behind Ty's warehouse, Ty helped River out of the vehicle, and Lachlan helped them bring the painting inside. On the security screen, they watched until the SUV had driven down the alley and turned off onto the street.

Ty turned. "Computer, turn on the lights." As the lights blinked on, he glanced at River. "You all right?"

She nodded. She felt tired to her bones.

"Why don't you take a shower? I'll find some clothes for you, and make us something to eat." He carefully set the painting's storage box on a bench in his lab. He clicked the box open and pulled the painting out.

She tilted her head. "You look awfully calm for a man handling four hundred and fifty million dollars."

"I'm good with my hands."

She smiled. "I know."

His dark eyes caught hers. "Go and shower, River. Otherwise, if you stand there looking at me like that, I'm going to fuck you on the floor."

Every cell inside her body flared to brilliant life.

"River."

Licking her lips, she headed down the hallway to the bedrooms. She hesitated for a second, then walked into Ty's room. The adjoining bathroom was gorgeous. It was filled with dark, glossy stone, and chrome taps. For some reason, the dark elegance of it reminded her of the man who owned it. It looked glossy, hard, and cold, but—she flicked on the water in the large shower and steam rose up—beneath it was heat.

She stripped off her dusty, dirty gear, dropping it on the floor. Then she stepped under the spray and let the water wash the blood and dust away.

CHAPTER TEN

Ty finished cooking the chicken stir-fry. He didn't cook much, but as a kid, his parents' chef had showed him how to make a few meals. Usually on nights when Ty had been lonely and snuck out of bed.

He lifted the pan off the stove. "Computer, any messages?"

"Yes," the bland voice told him. "There is a message from your father."

Wonderful. Ty's jaw tightened. "Play message."

"Ty." His father's deep voice. "Your mother wants to know if you'll make it to her birthday gala."

When hell froze over. The last thing he needed was his mother to invite every suitable Chicago debutante to parade in front of him.

"I know better than to ask about your work...since it's all classified."

Ty rolled his eyes.

"I also wanted to let you know that a position has

come up at Sampson Finance. My Head of Business Improvement is retiring. I think this would be a brilliant position for you. It would be challenging, and a way for you to take a place in your legacy."

Leaning against the counter, Ty dropped his head and looked at his bare feet. Same old story with his father.

"It's time to stop wasting your abilities, Tyler."

"Fuck off, Dad. Computer, end message." He sensed movement and looked up.

River stood in the doorway of his kitchen, her dark hair wet and looking far longer than it usually did. She was wearing one of his shirts, and the white fabric made her skin look darker.

"Hungry?" He knew that he was, and it wasn't for food.

She was silent for a second. "Famished."

He waved to the couch. "Sit. I'll bring it over."

She sat down, tucking her long legs under her. He served up the food and handed her a plate.

"Your father has no idea what you do," she said.

Ty sat down. "No. And don't be fooled, he wouldn't care even if he did."

"From the little I've seen, you do amazing work, Ty. You're indispensable to your team."

"If you aren't making millions, it isn't enough for my father." Ty stabbed a piece of chicken. "My grandfather was raised on the South Side of Chicago. He was a self-made millionaire who pulled himself out of poverty. My father takes great pride in continuing the legacy. I'm considered an oddity and a disappointment for not toeing the family line. Not living up to my potential."

"I'm sorry," she said quietly.

Ty just shrugged. "I don't let it bother me."

"Sure." She sounded like she didn't believe him. "I'm the illegitimate daughter of an earl. I don't let that bother me." Her nose wrinkled.

"Families suck."

She waved her fork. "Now, there is something we can agree on."

"People generally suck, as a whole."

"I'm not quite as jaded as you."

"Liar. How's your stab wound?"

"Healing up nicely." Her gaze moved to the bandage that peeked out from the neckline of the clean T-shirt he'd pulled on after his quick shower. "How's your shoulder?"

"Fine. I cleaned it again and put some of my special cream on it. It'll be much better in the morning."

"Another of your special inventions, huh?"

He sat down beside her. "I like fiddling around and making useful things."

She lifted her plate and breathed deep. "Including food. This smells good."

"Just a stir-fry. My skills don't extend too far in the kitchen."

"You'd prefer to be locked away in your lab, alone and brooding."

He cocked his head. "Hell, yeah."

She laughed and tucked into her food.

As they ate, Ty felt a tension between them. Not

uncomfortable or bad, but he was fully aware of every move she made. They'd both survived a near-death experience, which had ended with him yanking her panties down and giving her an orgasm.

He saw she'd swiveled and was looking into his lab. He followed her gaze, and saw the painting on the bench.

"We can take a closer look at the *Salvator Mundi* in the morning."

She nodded. "I'll need to let my client know we recovered it."

"First, we need to decode the map. We have to make sure the painting isn't dangerous."

"Maybe the orb is harmless?" she said. "Maybe it was destroyed centuries ago?"

Ty had seen too much damage from powerful artifacts. They couldn't risk making those assumptions. "How about we take a look at it now?"

She smiled and nodded. She leaned forward and set her empty plate on the coffee table. Ty followed her into the lab, dropping onto a stool in front of the painting. River pressed her hands to the edge of the bench and leaned forward.

It was amazing to think that this had all been hidden under someone else's bad paintwork for centuries. His gaze fixed on the orb.

It was definitely strange that da Vinci hadn't painted the light refraction correctly. The three brightest spots on the orb seemed to glow. They looked like twinkling stars.

"These bright spots stand out," River said.

Ty grunted.

"I read one theory that people think the dots represent a constellation."

Ty made a cross noise. "Every conspiracy theory tries to align anything old with a damn constellation."

She laughed, a deep, sexy sound. As she shifted closer, her fresh scent reached him—freshly showered skin and his own damn soap. He tried to rein in his desire.

They'd both had a hell of a night and needed some rest.

"I'll take some high-res images of the dots and run them through my databases. And in the morning, we'll check in with Nat. See if there are any references to the orb in the da Vinci codices she's been studying."

River leaned against the bench. "It's nice having the backup and help of a team."

"Yeah, it's not so bad."

"They're loyal to you. And you're loyal to them."

Ty hopped off the stool. "I know they have my back."

"Oh, they do."

He grabbed her arm. "Someone giving you a hard time?"

"They're just being protective."

He scowled. "Who?"

River smiled. "I can protect myself, Mr. Scientist."

"I know that." He grabbed one of her curls, rubbing it between his fingers. It didn't stop these damn inconvenient feelings of wanting to protect her, though. "Time for us to sleep."

He headed back toward the kitchen, scooping up the

dirty plates off the coffee table. He dumped the plates in the sink.

"We need to rest and recharge, so we can hit our work hard in the morning."

He turned and went as still as a statue.

River stood in the center of his living room. She'd unfastened the buttons on his shirt, baring her naked body beneath.

He sucked in a breath, desire slamming into him like a crashing plane.

POTENT NEED COURSED THROUGH RIVER. She wasn't shy about her body, and she loved watching the hunger and appreciation fill Ty's handsome face.

His gaze roved over her. Her skin felt hot and tight. She wanted him so bloody bad.

Hell, she'd wanted him from the moment he'd caught her breaking into his place. And she was sick of fighting it.

They'd almost been killed tonight, and now she wanted to remember that they were both very much alive.

His dark eyes were on her as he crossed the room.

He swept her into his powerful arms. He spun, and a second later, her butt hit the dining room table.

"You've had no panties on all this time?" he growled.

"Nope."

He dropped to his knees and nudged her thighs apart.

All River had time to do was suck in a breath, then his mouth was on her.

She cried out, gripping the edge of the table.

"Wanted my mouth right here when we were in that vault," he growled. "Wanted my tongue inside you, your honey on my lips."

White-hot desire raged through her. She held on, tilting her hips up to meet his mouth. He was ruthless, working her with his tongue and lips. His goatee rubbed against her sensitive flesh.

She heard husky cries, and realized the needy, hungry sounds were coming from her. She reached for something to anchor her, sliding her hands into his hair. She pressed harder against him.

"I like it harder," she gasped.

His tongue dove inside her. He increased the pressure, then moved and sucked her clit into his mouth.

River let out a cry and wrapped her legs around his head. She heard herself moaning. A moment later, it was like being hit by an inferno. Her back arched and she cried out as she came.

Oh. God. The sensations were too much, not enough. Her body shook hard.

She was barely conscious or capable of thought when Ty pulled his mouth off her and stood. She watched as he shoved his sweatpants down and then she heard the crinkle of a packet.

The muscles in her belly clenched in anticipation. *Yes.* She wanted this man. All of him.

Then his big body was pressing up against hers, and she wrapped her legs around his hips.

With one single thrust, he lodged his hard cock inside her.

God. "Ty!"

"Finally." He let out a deep groan.

"Yes."

He started with hard, heavy thrusts. She felt possessed, owned. Her nails dug into his biceps.

"I've wanted you since you climbed out my window." His voice was a deep rumble.

River cried out again. Then Ty pushed her down onto the table. As his hips kept plunging, his hands caressed her body. They moved over her breasts, then higher to cup her shoulders. He used the grip for leverage and kept hammering inside her.

"You like that?" he growled. "You like my cock inside you?"

"Yes." His face looked harsh, hard. Like a god taking what was his.

"I love how tight you feel. How wet you are."

"I'm wet any time I look at you," she confessed.

He growled and increased the pace.

River tried to hold on, fighting to hold back the whirling sensations as her next orgasm rushed at her.

But it was too much. She reared up, her nails scratching down his back as she came. "Ty!"

He grunted, and with his next thrust, he came hard inside her.

River blinked. She was pretty sure she couldn't see. All she could hear was the harsh sawing of their breaths.

"Your shoulder okay?" she asked.

"What shoulder?"

She laughed. God, she'd never laughed when a man's cock was still lodged inside her before. "Is it wrong that I feel more shaken now than when that damn bomb went off?"

Ty barked out a laugh and pulled out of her. The move sent small quivers through her body.

"Well, nice job fucking my brains out," she said.

"Oh, I'm not done. I'm just getting started."

She shivered, and he scooped her up off the table.

As he carried her to his bedroom, River reminded herself that this was just shagging. They'd get their fill of each other, enjoy it, then walk away. Whatever happened, she knew she couldn't let herself forget that.

CHAPTER ELEVEN

She was laid out in his bed, her curls spread across his pillows and her gorgeous body under his hands.

Ty was taking his time worshiping River. He moved his mouth over her breasts, sucking one nipple between his lips.

She writhed beneath him. "Cock, now."

"Patience." He peppered her skin with more kisses.

She writhed again. *So impatient.* She reached for his cock.

"Get to the fucking," she complained.

He pushed up on his knees and moved over her. His cock slid through her folds and he bit back a groan. Damn, she felt good. He listened to her moan.

"How do you want it?" he rasped.

"Hard."

He rubbed against her again.

"And now," she choked out. "Or I'll tie you up and take it."

His gut clenched. He loved when she talked tough. "You like to play, River?"

She stilled, and fire lit in her pale-brown eyes. "I'm always game for new things. And I'm good with knots."

Fuck. She was perfect. He slid inside her.

She moaned. She couldn't stay still, and started rocking up to meet his thrusts.

He grabbed her wrists and pinned her arms above her head. He pushed them down into the bed and she pushed up against him.

"You're right where I want you," he murmured.

She tried to shove him off, but he held her down. Her lips parted. "God, Ty. I'm so close."

She liked him holding her down. He kept thrusting inside her, enjoying the tight clasp of her body. "Come for me, River."

She cried out, her body clenching tight on his. He kept thrusting through her orgasm, gritting his teeth to hold his own in check. But he couldn't hold back. She was so slick and wet. She felt like heaven.

Ty thrust deep again and started to come. He grunted through the waves of sensation.

Wrung out, he let her wrists go. He lifted one and pressed a kiss to it.

"Be right back." He slid off the bed and she made a small, throaty sound that made him smile. He went to the bathroom to get rid of the condom and wash his hands.

When he came back, she was standing beside the bed.

He stopped and arched a brow. She was wearing his lab coat. It wasn't fastened, giving him a teasing view of the breasts he'd just worshipped, the belly he'd just caressed, and the neatly waxed mound between her thighs.

His cock twitched again. Damn, he felt like he was a teenager again.

Then she snapped something between her hands. His gaze sharpened. She'd gotten one of his ties from his closet.

"My turn," she purred.

He raised a brow. "You want to tie me up? Again?"

"Yeah, but this time, we'll have more fun." She lowered her eyelashes. "And after, you can return the favor."

Ty sucked in a breath. "I'm pretty sure you know all the tricks on how to escape."

"I'll teach you."

He closed the distance between them and cupped her face.

"Do you trust me?" she whispered.

"I shouldn't, I don't trust many people."

They stared at each other.

"But yeah, I do," he murmured.

He saw something flare in her eyes. "Get on the bed."

Ty obeyed, leaning back against the headboard, and propping a pillow behind his head. It was almost identical to the last time she'd tied him to the bed.

When he looked up, her gaze was sliding down his naked body. Yeah, this time was going to be a lot more fun.

"River?"

Her gaze jerked up to his and she put one knee on the

bed. As she leaned over, her breasts bobbed in front of his face. She expertly tied him to the headboard.

She leaned back, running her hands down his chest. He jerked toward her, but the binding held him fast.

Then she pressed her lips to the center of his chest. "All mine. All this sexy man spread out for my pleasure."

He groaned. She took her time, worshiping him like he'd worshipped her.

Then she moved lower. And lower.

The muscles in his gut tensed. She dragged her tongue over the ridges of his abdomen, then moved lower still.

When she gripped his thick cock, he pulled in a sharp breath. "River—"

She made a humming sound, then sucked his cock between her lips.

Fuck. His hips bucked up, his groan strangled.

"You're so gorgeous." She murmured against the head of his cock. "Big, built, beautiful. I love your body. You're sexy as hell, Dr. Sampson."

She sucked him deeper, bobbing up and down as she took as much of his cock in her mouth as she could.

"Enough." His voice was barely understandable. He jerked on the tie. "*River.*"

She lifted her head, her tongue circling the swollen head of his cock. "I'm not finished."

"I'm going to come, so do you swallow?"

She smiled, her fingers wrapping around him, and she started pumping his cock. "Come for me, Ty. I want to watch."

He watched her pretty fingers on him, working him

hard. It didn't take long before his orgasm hit and his hips bucked.

"Fuck, River." He started coming, spilling on his belly, come splattering on his skin.

River watched, still stroking, enraptured.

Finally, Ty slumped back against the headboard. She slid up beside him and snuggled against his side.

He went still, enjoying the affectionate move. He didn't think River was a cuddler. Hell, he wasn't a cuddler.

"We need some sleep," he murmured.

She nodded.

"You going to untie me?"

She smiled. "Maybe."

He pressed a kiss to her temple. "I need to clean up and then it's time to sleep. I'm exhausted."

"Need your sleep, old man." With a flick of her wrist, Ty was free.

"Good sleep is essential to good health."

He shot her a smile as he headed for the bathroom. When he returned, he slid into the bed, pulled her close, and flicked the lamp off.

"Sleep."

"Okay, Ty." She rested her head on his chest.

He nuzzled his face against her hair. "I like you, River. A lot."

She didn't reply, but went very still, then she snuggled deeper against him.

RIVER FINISHED EATING her French toast and set her knife down on her plate. She groaned. She was bursting at the seams, but every mouthful had been so good.

"All done?" Ty asked, from the other side of the kitchen island.

She nodded.

"A night of good sex, a few hours of solid sleep, and now a world-class breakfast." She licked her lips. She wasn't embarrassed to admit she felt a few interesting twinges throughout her body. "What more does a woman need?"

His eyes narrowed. "*Good* sex?"

She smiled and waggled her eyebrows. "Pleasurable, decent, passable."

He gave a mock growl and River almost laughed. God, when was the last time she'd played with a man? Teased him?

"Guess I'll have to refresh your memory," he said. "Now, go to the bedroom and take all your clothes off."

Her head shot up. His voice was deep, with a growly edge. He was staring at her, gaze hot and intense.

How she'd ever thought this man was cool was beyond her. He raised a dark brow, and a shiver ran through her. They'd already had a lot of sex. And he knew full well it was lightyears beyond good. They should both be incapable of another quiver of desire.

Her gaze dropped, and she saw that big cock was hard again, tenting the front of his sweats.

"River."

She rose, then turned and sauntered toward his

bedroom. She made sure she put a little extra swing in her hips. Her breathing was already fast, her pulse jumping.

With each step, River realized that she trusted Ty Sampson. She'd let him strip her, and she'd let him tie her up. She shrugged out of her borrowed shirt and climbed onto the bed. She raised her arms above her head.

He came into the room and she felt his presence like an impending storm. His eyes flared.

"So beautiful." He grabbed the tie she'd used on him earlier and ran it through his hands.

River felt a rush of dampness between her thighs. She tried not to fidget.

He sat beside her hip and reached up. She took in that magnificent chest, itching to touch him again. He took her wrists and started tying her to the headboard.

With her arms stretched up, it lifted her breasts up. He trailed his fingers down the center of her body, and she arched into his touch.

"All mine to play with." He finished tying her hands.

She tested the bonds. He'd done a decent job. Then his fingers drifted over her skin, plucking at her nipples until she moaned. River's thoughts scattered.

"You have beautiful hands," she gasped out.

His white teeth flashed. "My hands are the tools of my trade."

He was methodical, touching everywhere he wanted. His blunt fingers circled her belly button. Then they dipped between her thighs, stroking.

"Ty."

"All mine." His fingers plunged inside her.

Husky cries broke from her throat. She couldn't move her arms, couldn't leave the bed, and yet, she felt safe. Was right where she wanted to be. This big, sexy man was taking his time to stroke her, touch her the way she liked best.

She'd never let go like this before. She'd never trusted anyone like this.

Ty took his time, torturing her by flicking at her clit, and driving his fingers deep inside her. He brushed a sensitive spot inside and she reared up. Like the scientist he was, he catalogued her every reaction, learning exactly what made her body strain against the bindings. He moved his fingers, stretching her.

"God, Ty."

Then his hand slipped away. He reached up and untied her.

She frowned. "No—"

"Shh." A guttural order.

River looked into his face and froze. His cheekbones looked more prominent, his eyes a little feral. A man on the edge.

He gripped her and spun her around. She found herself on all fours on the bed. He shoved a pillow beneath her hips, then he reached for her wrists. He pulled them into the small of her back so she tipped forward on the pillow. With several quick moves, he tied her hands behind her.

Anticipation licked at her like hot flames.

"This ass." His hands shaped over her buttocks. He kneaded the flesh.

She made a hungry moan. She should have been

embarrassed, but she wasn't, instead, she was delirious with desire.

"I want to see my handprint turn your ass cheek pink."

God. River shifted. She'd never let anyone spank her before. She felt a rush of wet between her legs.

"You want that?" he asked, fingers toying with the base of her spine.

She shoved back against him. "Yes."

Smack.

The blow was a surprise and she jerked. He hit her again. *Smack.*

God. Sensation spiked inside her and she dug her knees into the bed. He wasn't hitting her hard, just firm enough for her to feel it. Then she felt his fingers between her thighs again. She rocked against him. *Yes.*

He stroked, then withdrew. He spanked her again, and again. Each blow didn't hurt, but a tingling, burning sensation spread over her skin, and her belly coiled tight. Soon, she was a mindless, trembling mass of need.

"Ty," she cried out.

"Right here, baby."

She heard the crinkle of the condom wrapper. A second later, his big body was behind her, and then his thick cock was sliding inside her.

She was tied up. Helpless, with no control. And she loved it. Because she was with him.

His hips hammered against her, their flesh slapping together.

"So tight, River. So hot."

She moaned.

"You should see the way your body loves my cock. I see it stretching around me, taking me deep."

Her belly coiled tighter. "I'm going to come," she panted.

"Me, too. Come, River." Even as he kept thrusting, his hand reached beneath her body. His fingers pinched her clit.

That was all it took. She screamed and threw her head back. Sensations ripped her apart and it felt like she was flying.

With a deep groan, Ty thrust inside her again and stayed there. Another deep growl came from him as he poured himself inside her.

Then he dropped to the bed beside her. She felt the brush of his fingers at her back, but River's fingers gave a small flick and the tie around her wrists loosened. Her hands flopped to the bed.

He smiled. "Should've known you could get out in a flash."

He lay sprawled beside her, stretched out like some king, or an emperor.

"Handy to know how to do that," he said.

River felt lazy, satiated, and so good. "I'll show you how."

She pushed up to sit and grabbed the tie. She wrapped it around his thick wrists.

When she looked at him, she saw he was staring at her naked breasts. "First, you need to concentrate on the job."

Dark eyes met hers and he smiled. "Impossible with you naked beside me."

"Focus, Dr. Sampson. You have an incredible brain in there, I'm sure you can manage."

She leaned down and kissed the inside of his wrist. Sidetracked, she let her mouth move over his skin. She loved the salty taste of him.

Then she sat back, showing him how to work the binding loose. He followed her instructions—no surprise that he was a quick learner—and a second later, the tie fell from him.

"You're a natural." She grinned at him.

"I want to know all your secrets," he murmured.

River's heart thumped against her ribs, her smile dissolving. She'd never told anyone her secrets. For the first time in her life, she was tempted. Some part of her wanted to tell him everything.

"You're safe with me," he said quietly.

"I look at you and it's like looking at a piece of myself." As soon as the words tumbled out, she felt silly. She tried to shake off the vulnerability.

"You already know everything about me," he said.

"It was my fault Jack died."

Ty stilled. "I don't believe that."

"I was too late, and he died in my arms."

Ty grabbed her arm. "Talk to me."

Emotions rose up, but with this man beside her she did feel safe. God, when had she ever felt someone had her back? Someone who would help fight her demons?

She met his gaze. "I told you Chadwick Alton was in London for an arms deal. Our team had been running an investigation for months. We were at the warehouse that day to take him and his local contact down." She paused, her stomach jumping. "Another agent on our team was bribed. He kept me busy so I couldn't get to Jack. I *should* have known better. I was too late."

Ty reached for her other arm, but she jerked back.

"The mission blew up in our faces. Alton got away. Jack died. Now his wife is a widow, and his kids are fatherless."

"River—"

"I was *nothing*. I have nobody, except a father who checks in when it suits him. A man who cheated on his wife and family." She shook her head. "It should have been me who died."

"Come here, River."

She shook her head.

"Here. Please."

Something in his voice penetrated. He sounded like he was just as mixed up about his need to comfort her.

She shifted toward him. He wrapped his arms around her and held her tight. She buried her face against his chest. Her eyes burned, but she didn't cry. River never cried.

"My parents..." His voice trailed off, then he cleared his throat. "As a kid, I knew all about hiding pain, burying it deep, and showing no vulnerability."

Her arms convulsed. He liked to say it was easy not to care, to dislike people. But even when the pain was hidden, it didn't mean that the pain wasn't there, that you didn't feel it.

Eventually, she pulled back. "Sorry." She swiped a hand under her nose. "I'm under control now. I didn't mean to fall apart."

"Dealing with your feelings shows strength." He stroked one of her curls. "You can't blame yourself."

She lifted her chin, pushing her hair back from her face. "I'm fine."

"Have you ever talked to anyone about Jack's death?"

She shook her head. "Opening up..."

"Feels like stripping naked and standing in the middle of a crowd?"

Her lips quirked and she nodded.

"I'm glad you talked to me." He dropped a kiss to her lips. "Very glad. Now, I need to clean up and shower. Then we have a mysterious painting to solve."

River nodded. Work. That was exactly what she needed right now.

Ty climbed out of the bed, his fantastic, tight ass on display. Unashamed, she watched him disappear into the bathroom.

Then she let out a shaky breath. Hell, she'd just cracked herself open and spilled her secrets. She wondered if Ty Sampson was good for her health. She pulled in a jagged breath. *What the hell are you doing, River?*

CHAPTER TWELVE

W ith a cup of coffee in his hands, Ty sat on a stool in his lab and studied the *Salvator Mundi*.

He heard quiet footsteps, and River appeared, fresh from the shower and once again, wearing one of his shirts.

She moved up behind him, leaning down to brush her lips against the side of his neck. When he turned his head, she looked almost surprised that she'd made the move.

Up close, he smelled the fresh scent of her, and his cock stirred. *Shit*. His gaze dropped, taking in the long length of her bare legs. His body should need to recover, but he wanted her again.

"Coffee's fresh," he said.

Her nose wrinkled. "You have any tea?"

"Probably."

He watched her saunter away, loving the way she moved. He watched her rummage around in his kitchen and smiled. With a start, he realized that he didn't mind River being in his space. In fact, he sort of liked it.

Turning, he scowled at the painting, trying to push that feeling away. Soon, River was back with a steaming mug of black liquid. She took a sip and hummed.

Yep, his cock was hard again.

"Find anything?" she asked.

He shook his head. "I'm running searches on the pattern of dots on the orb."

She tilted her head, looking at the dots. "They really do look like stars. Could it be a constellation?"

Ty rolled his eyes. "All good crackpot conspiracy theories go for stars, constellations, and aliens."

She laughed. "All those crackpot theories are floating around because clearly, what they teach about history isn't quite correct. People are trying to fill in the gaps they know are there."

He grunted. "Maybe, but I can assure you that aliens had nothing to do with building the pyramids, or that." He nodded at the painting.

Perching on a stool, she jiggled one foot. "So, we can scratch off stars, then?"

He let out a huff of air. "Well, apparently a lot of people think those three dots match the constellation of Leo."

She sipped her tea. "So, it was aliens."

He shot her a look. "Based on three dots, I'm not buying it. Besides, even if they did match Leo, what the hell would that prove?"

"The dots must be something related to da Vinci."

"Nat's going to call any minute now." He thumbed

his tablet screen, propping it up on the bench. "Maybe she's had more luck."

A moment later, the screen flickered, and Nat's attractive face appeared. "Hi." The archeologist looked fresh and styled. Her gaze flicked between Ty and River, then her eyes widened and she grinned. "So, you guys look...refreshed. And River is wearing your shirt."

"Don't start, Nat," Ty growled.

"The team is going to *love* this."

"Mysterious orb to find," Ty reminded her.

"Right." She attempted to school her face into a more serious expression. "Are you guys okay? Lachlan told me about the bomb."

"We're alive."

"A man of few words, as always," Nat said dryly. "You'll be happy to hear that I found something."

Ty felt a rush of excitement. It was the same feeling he got whenever he made a new discovery in his lab. River leaned forward, pressing against his arm.

"I found a reference to da Vinci's orb in the Codex *Arno*," Nat said with a flourish.

"What does it say?" River asked.

"Well, it seems the orb is filled with a liquid."

Ty sat back. *A liquid?* "Go on."

"Did you know that da Vinci's mentor, the man he apprenticed under for years, was an accomplished alchemist?"

"Alchemist." River tilted her head. "That's the Elixir of Life and the Philosopher's Stone, right?"

Ty raised a brow. "Right."

She sniffed. "I watched *Harry Potter*."

Nat laughed. "Alchemy was a precursor to modern chemistry, with a dash of the occult thrown in."

"Charlatans," Ty grumped.

He watched Nat and River share a grin.

"So, Da Vinci's mentor, Andrea del Verrocchio, was an alchemist," Nat continued, "and there's some speculation that da Vinci was as well. Da Vinci apprenticed in his workshop from age fourteen."

"And he came up with whatever the hell this liquid is inside the orb," River said. "Could it be the Elixir of Life?"

Nat's nose wrinkled. "The Elixir and the Philosopher's Stone are the most well-known items when it comes to alchemy, but there are no references to either of those in da Vinci's codices."

"They were said to give immortality, right?" River asked.

Ty groaned. "That's all we need, some liquid that would give Alton immortality."

"Actually," Nat said, "the main stories around the Elixir and the Philosopher's Stone said that they turned metal into gold. That was the whole drive behind alchemy, transforming one metal into another."

Ty nodded. "That could be a valuable thing to get your hands on."

River shrugged. "Alton is a billionaire already. How many more billions does he need?"

"People do a lot of shit for money," Ty said.

"Da Vinci does mention something else in the codex," Nat said. "A brief mention, then nothing."

Ty and River leaned forward.

"He calls it the Gift."

"What is it?" Ty asked.

"I believe the fluid in the orb can help someone transform. Da Vinci drank it."

"What's it do?" River asked.

Nat ran a hand through her hair. "I'm making some assumptions here, but I believe it turns someone into a genius."

Ty hissed out a breath.

River's eyes went wide. "How's that possible?"

Nat's face lit up as she talked. "He talks about opening pathways, stimulating the brain."

Ty shook his head. "You think da Vinci created this elixir, the Gift? And took it?"

"He was an illegitimate child of a notary." Nat sat back. "He had a very unremarkable childhood and then a pretty standard apprenticeship with Verrocchio. Then, in his twenties, he had a veritable explosion of ideas and genius. And not just in one discipline," Nat continued. "Painting, science, design, engineering, geology, anatomy. He's now known as the best example of the Universal Genius or Renaissance Man. A polymath with expertise in several fields."

Ty thrust a hand through his hair. "Okay. So maybe the orb holds a fluid that can turn someone into a genius. Anything else in the codices, Nat?"

The archeologist shook her head. "But I'll keep looking. Da Vinci was working for the Medici at the time he made the Gift. The Medici family were the wealthiest family in Florence. Lorenzo de' Medici was famous for sponsoring lots of scholars and artists. From my research,

Leonardo was probably living in one of several of the Medici villas sprinkled around Florence and the hills. My guess is somewhere near Fiesole, just north of Florence. It's where he's said to have tested his theories of flight." She smiled. "By strapping some wings on an assistant and making him jump off a hill. Sounds like something you'd do, if you could, Ty."

Ty grunted and River didn't bother to hide her grin.

"Luckily, the poor guy survived," Nat continued. "I'm going to focus my attention on searching for anything from that time."

"Thanks, Nat."

She nodded and blinked off.

Fiesole. Something tweaked inside Ty's head, but he couldn't quite grasp the thought.

"Ty? I can see you thinking. It's kind of sexy."

He glanced at River. "Don't distract me." He pulled his laptop over and started typing. "Something about Fiesole." He pulled up information on the town, just a few miles northeast of Florence, nestled in the hills. He stilled. In his mind, images swirled.

"Are you having a wave of genius?" River leaned over his shoulder. "Without even having had any elixir?"

He shot her a look. The laptop beeped. "Hell."

Taking in his serious tone, she stepped back, looking at the laptop. "What?"

"The dots on the orb match locations around Florence."

She blinked. "What?"

"I used the town of Fiesole as one dot and triangulated and extrapolated distances. The other two dots match the town of Vinci, where Leonardo was born, and the final dot is the *Palazzo Vecchio* in the center of Florence. The town hall."

"I've visited the *Palazzo Vecchio*. Da Vinci painted something in there."

"Yes, the *Battle of Anghiari*. He and rival Michelangelo had a painting contest. Michelangelo was tasked to paint another wall of the same room. Unfortunately, the techniques Leonardo used failed and the fresco melted." Ty tapped on the screen. "The most well-known thing about the *Palazzo Vecchio* is that Michelangelo's *David* stands out at the front of it. Or it did. The one in the square is now a replica, and the real one is now in the *Galleria dell'Accademia* museum."

River frowned. "Okay, what's it all mean?"

"No idea." Ty crossed his arms. "Da Vinci and Michelangelo were said to be bitter rivals, and da Vinci's painting there was a failure, so I have no idea why he'd mark that location on the orb." Ty typed on the screen. "I'll keep running some searches and send this off to Brooks to do the same. He's better at this stuff."

"I have to say, I like it when you're being smart and geeky."

Ty grabbed her and she wrapped her arms around his neck. He lifted her onto the bench.

"The searches could take a while." He nudged her legs apart.

With a smile, she leaned forward and kissed him.

RIVER WOKE, stretching her arms over her head. The late-morning sun was shining through the window and across the bed. The sheets were empty, but smelled of Ty.

She smiled. She felt good. She'd never been one to laze around, but she decided she could get used to it, if it was in Ty's bed.

Finally, she pulled her lazy ass out of the bed and tugged on one of Ty's shirts. Wandering out of the bedroom, she found him in the lab. No surprise there.

He looked focused, and watching him made her feel a rush of heat in her belly. His brow was creased, and he looked his intimidating best.

She liked him. A lot.

She liked being with him. Licking her lips, she felt a flash of fear mixing with the desire inside her. She had to remind herself that this was temporary. When this mission was over, she was leaving.

"Hey?"

His deep voice made her look up. He was watching her.

She shook off her thoughts and smiled. "Any break-throughs?"

He scowled. "No."

"You still think these locations are important?"

"Yes."

His tablet chimed and when River glanced over, she saw Nat and Brooks' faces appear on the screen. Brooks was eating a bagel and, unfortunately, River couldn't see what was on his T-shirt today.

"Hi." Nat waved a slender hand.

Brooks gave them a chin lift.

Ty leaned forward. "I found something, Nat. The dots on the orb match locations around Florence." He briefly explained the three locations.

Nat tapped a nail against her chin. "So Vinci, Fiesole, and the *Palazzo Vecchio*? The orb, or at least a clue to the orb could be at any one of those locations."

Brooks nodded. "If I wanted to hide a clue to something important, I'd do it in a place that people would least expect."

River straightened. "Like on a statue made by a rival who you hate?"

Ty stiffened like he'd been electrocuted. "On the statue of *David*. Da Vinci and Michelangelo reportedly hated each other."

Nat smiled. "Does this mean we get a trip to Florence?"

Ty's gaze narrowed. "Maybe not. There's an exact replica of *David* right here in Las Vegas."

River raised her eyebrows. "There is?"

He nodded. "At Caesar's Palace."

"I'll call Lachlan," Brooks said. "Have the team meet you there."

River and Ty dressed quickly, and soon were in his Lexus heading toward Caesar's Palace. As they pulled in and parked, she saw the rest of Team 52 near the main entrance of the casino.

She climbed out of the car. "You really think it's possible that the orb is still wherever da Vinci hid it? After all these centuries?"

Ty glanced at her over the roof of his car. "Possibly.

I've seen some pretty crazy stuff when it comes to ancient artifacts. You'd be surprised what can survive the passage of time."

As they headed toward the others, River took in the casino's architecture. She'd never been to Caesar's Palace before. She frowned. It was a real mishmash of different styles—Roman, Greek, Renaissance. She shook her head. She had a hard time believing anything here could be a genuine replica.

The others were dressed in jeans and casual clothing, but River strongly doubted anyone would mistake them for tourists heading in to gamble. They radiated an aura that said they were all badass and trained to kill.

"There are two statues of *David* at Caesar's Palace," Lachlan said. "There's a large one in the Appian Way Shops, and a smaller one right here near the entrance."

Blair raised a brow. "I've always said bigger is better."

That got her a few snorts. As a group, they headed through the casino.

Axel grinned at them. "So, Ty, you and our ex-MI6 badass, huh?"

"Shut it," Ty said.

"Oh, no." Axel shook his head, his longish brown hair falling over his forehead. "I'm going to get a lot of mileage out of this."

"I could kill you in your sleep," River said silkily.

Axel's grin widened. "You could try, *chiquita*."

"Remember, I left you on your arse once before."

Axel shook a finger at her. "I won't underestimate you again."

"Who I fuck is none of your business," Ty grumbled.

"So, that's all this is?" Axel teased.

River turned and raised a brow. "Yep. We're just fucking each other's brains out, no strings attached."

Axel sighed. "Lucky bastard."

They reached the casino's shops, and ahead, she saw white marble pillars. It was hard to miss the statue. It was surrounded by arches and centered under a domed roof. Light shone down from a huge skylight. They circled around the front of it, and she had to admit, it was a pretty good replica.

"It's carved from the same Carrara marble that Michelangelo used," Ty said.

They all looked carefully at the stone.

"Queen Victoria was given a plaster cast of the original *David* as a gift from the Duke of Tuscany," Ty added. "Apparently, she was so shocked at his nudity, that she had a fig leaf commissioned to cover his attributes."

Callie snorted.

Blair crossed her arms. "He's a little slender for my liking."

Callie snorted again.

"Anyone see anything?" Lachlan asked.

River studied the smooth marble. She couldn't argue that Michelangelo had pulled off an amazing feat and created a gorgeous representation of a young, muscular biblical hero. But she didn't spy anything that could be a clue leading to da Vinci's orb.

Everyone shook their heads.

"Maybe we're wrong about it?" River muttered.

Which would leave them back at square one. They'd likely have to go to Italy and search the three locations.

"Take photos of it," Lachlan said. "From every angle. We'll study the images back at the Bunker."

Axel and Blair pulled out cameras and got to work. But River glanced at Ty and noted his tight jaw. All around, she felt the air of frustration from the team. It matched her own.

CHAPTER THIRTEEN

Ty preferred his own lab to the makeshift one at the Bunker. Nothing was quite how he liked it.

Pictures of the statue of *David* were laid out over every inch of the workbench. He reached for his coffee mug, sipped, and grimaced. It was stone cold. Sighing, he sat back and rubbed the bridge of his nose. He wasn't sure where River was. Probably somewhere having a stare-off with Blair.

He rubbed his tired eyes next. That was what a night of amazing sex got you. He smiled to himself. Not that he was complaining. He reached into his bag and pulled out the glasses that he rarely used and slipped them on.

He stared at the photos again. There was nothing on the statue that was giving him any clues, *dammit*.

The door swung open and River came in. She jerked to a stop and stared at him.

"What?" He frowned at her.

"You wear glasses?"

He shrugged a shoulder. "When I'm tired."

She moved closer. "They look hot."

Ty felt a curl of desire in his gut. He yanked her close and pressed a kiss to her lips.

She touched his glasses. "Very sexy, Professor Sampson." She rubbed against him. "I think I need to make an appointment with you to talk about my grades."

He grinned, that desire flaring hotter. "I've been very disappointed in your effort with your studies, Ms. Elliott-Hall."

"I can do better. I promise."

He liked seeing her play like this. "I know, and I'll let you show me just how good you can be. Later." He kissed her again.

There was the sound of a throat clearing and they both glanced up. Blair stood in the doorway, scowling at them. "Find anything?"

Ty shook his head. "No."

Blair sniffed. "I don't think the answer is in River's tonsils."

"Chill, Mason," River said. "I get that you're a badass and protective of your team, but I'm not going to hurt him, or any of your guys."

Blair folded her arms across her chest.

"I agreed to work with you," River added. "That means I'm on your side."

Blair looked at her for a long second. "You hurt him, and I'll hurt you." She swiveled and walked out.

"She's a bit of a bitch," River said.

"No, she's just an overprotective badass and a good friend."

147

River blew out a breath. "I know."

"It's what friends do," Ty said.

She lifted a shoulder. "I wouldn't really know." She looked down to where he'd been writing some notes regarding the statue of *David*.

"Maybe the statue at Caesar's Palace isn't an exact replica," she said.

"Maybe."

She glanced over his notes, then she straightened. "Wait. It says here that the statue of *David* looked toward Rome."

Frowning, he leaned over her shoulder and checked the notes. "Right. Toward the south."

River looked up, her face lighting up. "Anything related to da Vinci along that route?"

Ty quickly pulled up a map of the area on his laptop. He dragged a finger from the center of Florence along the direction to Rome. He stopped. "Nothing that I can see."

She snapped her fingers. "Wait! Da Vinci hated Michelangelo. Check locations along that line to the *north*."

Ty nodded. "The opposite direction. Toward Fiesole." He drew a line and stopped on a location. "There's a villa near Fiesole."

"Nat said da Vinci worked up in the hills. Maybe it's where he lived when he created the orb!"

Ty tapped on the computer and quickly pulled up information on the villa. "Well, damn. It's the Villa Medici."

River sucked in a breath. "Owned by Leonardo's patron."

"The villa was sold a few years back. It was purchased by Mohs Corp."

River snatched up a tablet and started tapping as well. "Who is Mohs Corp.?"

He shook his head. "I don't know, but Brooks will be able to find out."

"Here." She tilted the screen. "I found a recent article about the villa. A local paper did an article about a big archaeological dig at the villa, right after this corporation bought it."

Ty scanned the text. "Local residents reported lights on at night, mysterious trucks moving in and out of the dig. They only used external workers, nobody local." He met her gaze. "They were looking for something."

"Shit."

Ty tapped on his tablet. "Brooks, I need you to look into Mohs Corp."

On screen, Brooks nodded, swiping on his own tablet. "Hmm, at first glance, it looks like it's owned by a tangled web of offshore companies." He cracked his knuckles. "Which happens to be my specialty."

"We think whoever owns that corporation was looking for the orb at the Medici Villa," Ty said.

"Then let's see who they are," Brooks said.

RIVER SAT at the desk poring over the data in front of her. Sexy geek Brooks was sitting next to her. He'd flown in from Area 52. Ty was on her other side.

They were briefing Team 52. Everyone was packed

into the Bunker's conference room. Lachlan was scowling, and River wondered idly if the man ever smiled.

"You think whoever bought this villa found the orb?" Lachlan repeated.

River nodded. "We think so. They conducted a dig, moved artifacts out, and then let the villa become a tourist attraction."

"Brooks?" Lachlan looked at the man. "Who's behind Mohs Corp.?"

"I'm still trying to unravel the companies involved. Whoever they are, they've left a convoluted trail. They're damn good, and have a lot of money to burn."

River shifted. "We have an account by a Florence local that *something* significant was removed from the villa. Lots of artifacts from the dig were donated to local museums, like statues, mosaics, vases." She straightened. "The man said that the couple who owned the villa were American."

"That was a nice find." Brooks fist-bumped her.

River shot everyone a rueful glance. "I just don't know who the hell they are."

"We'll find them," Ty said.

"Keep searching," Lachlan ordered.

They got back to work, powered by caffeine and several boxes of cupcakes that Blair had brought in. The hours ticked by, and the next time River looked up, the table was littered with empty coffee mugs, cake crumbs, candy bar wrappers, and empty plates.

Brooks had left some time ago to go and have a nap, and River felt tired, too. She stretched her arms above her head.

Ty was beside her, looking as focused as ever. She had to admire the man's stamina. She suspected he could research for days on end and never give up until he found the answer he was looking for. But she could tell that his muscles were tense.

She stood up and gripped his shoulders. She started to rub.

He lifted his head, and as she dug her fingers into his firm muscles, he groaned.

"We should take a break. Maybe take a nap like Brooks," she suggested.

"I hope that's code for fuck."

She grinned at him. "Yes, that's code for fuck."

His burning-hot gaze landed on hers. God, everything inside her reacted to that look. No one had ever made her feel like this.

How could she be terrified and on fire at the same time?

Suddenly, Brooks' computer beeped, and they both looked over at it.

River touched the keyboard and then she hissed. "No way."

A single company name was displayed on the screen.

"Hell." Ty pulled his stool closer, frowning.

"The villa was purchased by Diamond."

Ty shook his head. "Mohs is the hardness scale used to rate minerals, like diamond."

Diamond was the biggest tech company in the world. River's phone was made by Diamond, and she guessed Team 52 used some of their gear as well. In fact, she'd bet money that the laptop they were using had parts made by Diamond.

A decade ago, the company had revolutionized cell phones and personal computers. They'd made them cool, and added the best features.

All thanks to the company's genius founder, Sam Work.

The man had started the company in his garage, and had been known for his revolutionary ideas and passionate beliefs. By all accounts, he'd been arrogant, driven, and rude, but a visionary.

He'd died two years previously of cancer. He'd been called the genius of his generation.

River sucked in a sharp breath and locked gazes with Ty. "No way."

Ty leaned back. "Ordinary guy. He didn't excel at school, then *bam*, the man's full of cutting-edge, revolutionary tech ideas."

"You think Sam Work drank from da Vinci's genius orb?"

"It's possible."

The idea was mind-boggling. She tapped a finger on the bench. Even if Work had taken the da Vinci elixir, he'd used his ideas as a force for good, although it had amassed him enormous wealth.

River tapped on the computer. "When he died, Work left everything to his wife, Laura Work." Excitement vibrated through River. "She's pretty reclusive and refuses interviews. She lives in San Francisco." More tapping, and then River grinned as she looked at Ty. "And guess what else?"

"Tell me."

"Ty, she's rumored to have a *huge* art collection. She's said to have spent hundreds of millions of dollars on it."

"Jeez." He stroked his goatee. "Any da Vinci artifacts?"

"No one knows what exactly she has in her current collection. She refuses to show it, or tell anyone, and sellers have to sign non-disclosure agreements."

"So, there's no way to know for sure, but it's likely that she has the *Salvator Mundi* orb made by da Vinci in this massive collection."

River nodded. "Looks like we need to visit the Bay City."

CHAPTER FOURTEEN

Ty managed a few hours of sleep back at his place, wrapped around River. When his alarm went off, he bullied a grumbling River out of bed and into the shower.

Surprisingly, after a shower and a quickie with River's long legs wrapped around his waist and tight body milking his cock, Ty felt refreshed and energized. He watched as she dressed, and when she glanced his way, she smiled and winked.

She seemed miles away from the secretive, controlled woman he'd first met.

He watched as she pulled her tight curls back into a ponytail. He loved his hands buried in that hair and itched to tug that tie out.

"Come on," he said. "We'll be late to meet the others."

"Okay." She stopped and pressed her mouth to his neck. "By the way, I'm driving."

"No. My car, I drive."

Of course, she then used her mouth some more. Ty groaned, and felt her steal his car keys out of his pocket.

"Hey!"

She danced away, heading for his car. "Finders keepers, Sampson."

She drove several miles over the speed limit. Ty muttered under his breath the entire ride to the Bunker.

"I like your car." She pulled them to a stop.

"You're a pain in my ass."

She winked. "Arse."

He followed her inside and soon, the team was all assembled.

"Laura Work has the orb," Lachlan told them all.

Ty nodded. "From our research, she keeps an extensive art collection in her San Francisco mansion. That's where we think she'd keep the orb."

"So, we go in and get it," Blair said.

Ty shook his head. "It's not that simple."

Lachlan crossed his arms. "Go on."

On the screen on the wall, a picture of Work's house appeared.

Axel let out a low whistle.

It was a huge, modern house, with lots of angular glass and lights. It had a magnificent view of the bay.

"It was built a few years back, in the Pacific Heights area of San Francisco," River said. "There are no schematics for it on file."

"Okay." Seth was tapping his fingers on the table. "We can work around that."

River shook her head. "It's high-tech. Work has a top-of-the-line computer system running the entire house, including security. This is the definition of a house filled with Diamond technology. Unsurprisingly, she has one of the best security systems in the world."

The room filled with unhappy grunts.

"We're still trying to get our hands on more intel," Ty added. "All I know is that we can't break our way in. There is no way to break the encryption on the security system. Brooks has confirmed that."

"We could cut the power," Smith suggested.

Ty shook his head. "She has backup generators on site."

"Damn," Axel muttered.

Suddenly, the door flung open, and Brooks burst in. He looked disheveled, his red T-shirt—that had some logo on it and the words Rebel Scum emblazoned below it— was wrinkled. "I found something and it isn't good."

"Spit it out," Lachlan demanded.

"Chadwick Alton left for San Francisco an hour ago."

Everyone stiffened.

Ty scowled. *Fuck.* How the hell did the bastard know?

"There's no way that asshole put the pieces together himself," River said.

"Unless he got it from us." Ty scowled. "Either via a spy or a bug."

Lachlan lifted a finger to his lips.

Ty and Brooks leaped into action. Brooks started up a small sound distortion device that would hide what they said. Ty pulled out a scanner. They started sweeping the Bunker, testing for different frequencies.

In the main area, near Kinsey's desk, the scanner beeped.

"Found something," Ty said.

Nearby, Kinsey was frowning and wringing her hands.

Ty lifted a delivery box.

"That came in yesterday," she said. "It's just office stationery."

The scanner went crazy near one edge.

"Shit," Brooks muttered. "Looks like the bug is hidden in the packing tape. Ingenious."

Pissed, Ty checked it out. He nodded at Lachlan.

Lachlan picked up a notepad and pen. *Quarantine the bug. We'll feed him some misinformation.*

Brooks grinned and lifted the box. He headed down to the lower level, where they kept their soundproofed cells.

"Screw Alton," Lachlan said. "Time for *our* trip to San Francisco. Everyone gear up. We'll plan how to infiltrate Work's house on the X8."

"We need more information on the house, Lachlan," Ty said. "We can't go in blind."

"I'll get it," Lachlan said.

Ty frowned and glanced at River. She shrugged a shoulder.

"How?" Ty asked.

"I know someone in San Francisco. He's ex-military, and next-level badass."

Blair put one hand on her hip. "*We're* next-level badass."

Lachlan shook his head. "This guy has us beat. He's former Ghost Ops."

"Fuck," Seth muttered.

"You can say that again," Axel said.

Ty frowned. He'd heard rumors about Ghost Ops. The best of the best from all branches of the military's special forces, put together in a single team. A team who did the dirtiest, hardest, most classified jobs the government needed done.

"Norcross runs a private investigation and security firm in San Fran," Lachlan said. "He hired a bunch of former Ghost Ops men. Hell, he practically runs the damn city. If anything's going on in San Francisco, he knows about it."

Ty blew out a breath. He wasn't sure they wanted to tangle with this guy, let alone be indebted to him.

He looked at Laura Work's house again. But if the orb was in there, they needed to get in.

Then he looked at the woman by his side.

And he was beginning to realize that he'd do anything to ensure River's safety.

IT WAS OFFICIAL. River was in love with the X8, and she wanted one of her own.

As the jet-copter headed for San Francisco, she leaned over in her seat and looked into the cockpit. Blair and Seth made the high-tech controls look easy.

Blair could be an overprotective witch, but there was no doubting her piloting skills.

In the back of the aircraft, Ty had papers and his tablet spread out on the table between the seats. The others were sprawled around, checking weapons, or poring over the new data they'd received.

Lachlan's contact in San Francisco had come through.

Among the papers, River spotted a photo of Laura Work. River picked it up, studying the neat, attractive blonde who was in her early fifties.

"It's unlikely we can crack the security system." Axel tossed some papers down in disgust. "If this is correct, the fucking system is beyond top-of-the-line."

River had looked the intel over, and Axel was right. The system had enhanced Diamond components, and even Ty said he needed to see them in person to understand how they worked.

There was no way to easily crack the security. If they attempted it, they'd likely set off the alarms before they were even in the house.

River picked up another file filled with information. Whoever this guy was in San Francisco, he was good. He had a truckload of information on Work and her house. There were even several surveillance pics of the premises.

She studied one, seeing a cleaning crew entering the building. *Hmm*. She raised her hand. "Guys, we could go in as the cleaning crew. I almost did that at the Bunker."

"What?" Ty said. "You did?"

"I said I *almost* did." River rolled her eyes. "Work has her house cleaned twice a week by a large crew of cleaners. If we can sort it out, we could go in tomorrow."

Ty smiled. "That's genius."

She winked. "And I didn't even need to drink da Vinci's magic potion."

"Any updates on Alton?" Smith asked.

Lachlan shook his head. "Norcross and his men haven't seen him."

Hmm, River didn't like the sound of that. Alton was clearly out there, waiting in the grass like a snake.

When they landed at San Francisco Airport, two dark-gray SUVs were waiting.

As River followed Ty and the others off the X8, she looked up and stopped.

A man was leaning against the lead SUV.

"Yikes," Callie murmured from behind River.

Yikes, was right. River studied the man. He had his legs crossed at the ankles, his long limbs clad in trousers that had to be tailored for his big, muscled body. He wore a pale-blue business shirt, but had the sleeves rolled up, showing off muscular forearms. A shock of dark hair, that was just past needing a haircut, looked thick and a few shades off black. When he glanced their way, River sucked in a breath.

He was one of the most attractive men she'd ever seen. And she was currently surrounded by several who were pretty high on the hotness factor. The man by the SUV was nowhere near pretty, and maybe not even handsome, but his rugged face drew the eye, and it was hard to look away.

"Grade-A fantasy material there, ladies," Callie said.

"You aren't wrong," Blair agreed.

River nodded and saw Ty scowling at her. She smiled and patted his arm. "Just looking."

As they walked across the tarmac, she got close enough to see the man's eyes, and the breath rushed out of her chest.

Lachlan had a flat, assessing stare. She'd heard Blair describe it as a tiger's stare.

This man's eyes were even scarier than Lachlan's. At first, she thought they were brown, but up close, she saw they were a dark indigo blue. And as cold as the darkest depths of the North Sea.

Those eyes looked like he could see inside your head and extract your secrets...all while he killed with cold, methodical movements. He took them all in in seconds, and River was sure he'd catalogued every one of them.

Lachlan stepped forward and held out a hand. "Norcross."

The man straightened and shook Lachlan's hand. River noticed the tattoos on his arm, disappearing under the rolled up sleeves of his shirt.

"Hunter." A deep voice with a rough edge.

Lachlan turned. "This is my team. Everyone, I'd like you to meet Vander Norcross, owner of Norcross Security and Investigations."

River didn't scare easily, but as that dark-blue gaze swept over them and Norcross lifted his chin, she suppressed a shiver. It was official—the guy was as scary as hell.

Norcross handed over a slim black folder to Lachlan. "Everything else my team pulled together on Laura Work and her house."

Lachlan took the file. "Thanks."

"The SUVs are yours for the duration. If you need any backup, let me know and I'll activate my team."

River suspected Vander Norcross didn't need a team. The man could probably mow down an army of bad guys single-handedly.

"We also clocked Alton," Norcross added.

Lachlan straightened

"He and his team of goons got caught trying to break into Work's house today."

Shit. River glanced at Ty. He squeezed her arm.

Lachlan cursed. "And?"

"Most of his crew are sitting in a jail cell," Norcross said. "Alton and a couple of his guys got away. There's been no sign of them. Unfortunately, Work is now on high alert."

Dammit. River released a breath. Just what they didn't need.

Norcross gave them another cool sweep of his gaze, then a short nod. "Good luck."

"Thanks, Vander," Lachlan said. "I owe you."

"Any time, Lachlan." The man headed toward a sleek, BMW motorcycle parked nearby.

River stood with Blair and Callie, and they all watched Norcross swing a muscled leg over the bike. Then, the deep, throaty roar of the bike's engine sounded. Norcross pulled on a helmet, then tore away.

Callie let out a sigh.

"You can say that again," Blair murmured.

"Very interesting friends you keep, Hunter," River said.

"Pays to keep interesting friends around, MI6," Lachlan responded.

It didn't take Team 52 long to load into the SUVs. With Seth and Blair driving, San Francisco's landmarks whizzed past them.

They made their way to the exclusive Pacific Heights suburb. It was home to some of the city's most expensive real estate. River tried to guess how many billionaires, millionaires, and tech CEOs called it home.

They parked just down the road from Laura Work's mansion. Ty passed River a set of binoculars.

She lifted them, zooming in on the house. It was even more impressive in reality.

"I don't see any guards," Smith noted.

"She trusts her tech," Ty said. "And she has reason to."

"Definitely no easy way in," Blair said.

Lachlan nodded. "All right, time to pay Distinction Cleaning a visit. They're going to get themselves a new cleaning crew."

CHAPTER FIFTEEN

As soon as the white van pulled up to a stop in front of Laura Work's mansion, Ty slid the side door open.

Team 52 ducked out, everyone wearing white uniforms with the Distinction Cleaning logo on the chests.

He watched Blair, Callie, and Axel reach in, pulling out vacuum cleaners, mops, and buckets. Smith sat in the driver's seat. Since there was no way to make the big, muscular former SEAL look like a cleaner, he was staying in the van.

Lachlan had executed some fancy footwork with the cleaning company. That included the CEO of the company receiving a threatening phone call from Jonah. After that, they'd readily fallen in with Team 52's plan.

"Let's go," Lachlan said.

Hefting a mop onto his shoulder, Ty moved in beside River. She was clutching some dusters and cloths.

Lachlan coded them in through the front gate, and then they headed up the path toward the huge front doors.

Ty surreptitiously scanned their surroundings. Cameras were embedded everywhere. Laura Work was currently visiting one of her children, with Norcross providing surveillance to ensure she stayed away.

"No guards?" River asked.

Ty shook his head.

At the fancy lock at the door, they all used their key cards to swipe in, and then they were inside the building.

"Brooks," Lachlan murmured, standing beside an internal panel on the wall.

"Tapping into her system now," Brooks said through their earpieces. "Damn, it is one *hell* of a system. I'll only have partial control, but I'll do what I can. Cameras are down. I suggest you make this fast."

"Split up," Lachlan said.

The team broke apart, moving through the large living room and heading in different directions. Ty and River headed for the kitchen.

In his ear, he listened to the team steadily working through the house, clearing the rooms. He felt a niggle in his gut. They had no idea where the hell Chadwick Alton was.

"Where are you orb?" River murmured under her breath.

Ty and River stepped into an enormous and very white kitchen. The marble countertops gleamed white, threaded with gray. The modern appliances gleamed. He scowled. Something told him that Laura Work didn't have the orb hidden in her ovens or fancy fridges.

River pointed to a doorway. They moved into a secondary kitchen, clearly for staff, sitting behind the main one. More gleaming counters and cupboards. There were some steps that led down, and they moved into a storage area filled with neatly packed shelves of food.

"No orbs with the potatoes," River said, poking through some shelves.

"Maybe it's with the Pinot." He pointed to the floor. There was another set of stairs and a patch of floor made entirely of glass. It gave a clear view of the fancy wine cellar below. The large space was lined with built-in metal shelves, all filled with wine bottles.

Ty touched his ear. "We're heading down to the next level. A wine cellar."

"Acknowledged," Lachlan replied. "We're heading for the attic storage area."

Ty's boots echoed down the stairs as he stepped down into the wine cellar. River was right behind him as they walked along the shelves. They touched the bottles, searching for any sign of the orb.

She stopped and blew out a breath. "Nothing."

Ty stopped, shoving his hands on his hips. He studied the walls.

"What is it?" River asked.

In his head, he was doing some geometry. "The dimensions of this room are off."

She frowned. "It looks fine to me."

He glanced at the glass floor above, then back at the rows of wine. Maybe it was designed like this, but it felt like the far wall was too short. He remembered Alton's fancy, hidden wine room in his mansion. Ty walked over to the rack of wine, pressing his hands to the shelves.

Click.

Suddenly, the wall swung out and Ty stepped back.

Behind it was a staircase.

"Wow." River looked down. A set of wooden stairs disappeared into the gloom.

She reached into a pocket and pulled out a flashlight. Then, she took the first step down. Ty followed, his pulse jumping. This was it. He was sure of it.

They'd only taken a few steps when the door above them swung shut. It clicked closed, locking them in the dark stairwell.

"Shit." Ty pressed his hands to the door. It didn't budge and there was no lock, handle or panel. *Dammit.*

"Uh-oh," River said.

"Is that a professional MI6 term?"

"Yes. It means we're fucked."

Ty touched his earpiece. "Lachlan, River and I are headed down to some sort of basement room through the wine cellar. We're locked in."

No response.

"Lachlan? Lachlan?" Ty shook his head. "Dammit. No comms down here."

River nodded. "Let's check it out, then we can find a way out after."

She aimed her flashlight downward, the thin beam cutting through the darkness. They reached the bottom of the stairs, and Ty sensed the cavernous space ahead.

He stepped off the last step, his boot squeaking on a polished concrete floor.

Suddenly, automatic lights clicked on, and River gasped. Ty's chest went tight.

They were in some sort of underground garage. It was filled with cars. They were all parked in rows, at angles. It was a hell of a collection, an eclectic mixture of vintage and modern.

There was a mint-condition, Jaguar D-Type, several Aston Martins that looked like they belonged in old James Bond films, and some shiny red Ferraris from the 1960's. His gaze flicked to the far side of the basement, and he catalogued the modern cars: a Rolls Royce, two Lamborghinis, a Mercedes-Maybach, and two Bugattis. He looked at the back of a black Bugatti La Voiture Noire. He made a strangled sound. The vehicle was a thing of beauty—almost space-age looking, with quad tail pipes, and sleek, gorgeous lines.

River made a sound and he saw her rolling her eyes. "Put wheels on it, and it makes any man go gaga."

He grinned at her. "I still think you're more beautiful, but just so you know, that car—" he pointed at the Bugatti "—is worth just shy of nineteen million dollars."

Her eyes bugged out. "For a car?"

"I still think you're priceless, baby."

She poked her tongue out. "If you're done ogling the pieces of metal with wheels, we have something kind of important to find."

They wound their way through the cars. On one side wall, Ty noted several built-in storage closets. River moved to the first one and pulled the door open. They peered in. Definitely storage. He saw a bunch of ski gear.

They checked the other closets—mostly sports equipment, no sign of any artwork or artifacts. At the back of the basement, there was a blank cement wall. There were no doors and nothing attached to it.

River turned and shook her head. "Nothing. No artwork. No orb."

Ty shoved a hand through his hair. "Shit. Her art collection has to be here somewhere."

"Maybe the others have had better luck."

"You won't get the orb."

The male voice made them spin. The air caught in Ty's throat, and they watched as Chadwick Alton stepped out from behind one of the cars.

He aimed a handgun at Ty.

Two muscled thugs in tactical gear appeared behind him. They were armed as well.

"Now, I want you to find the orb for us Dr. Sampson, and then get us out of here," Alton said.

Ty raised a brow. "You know who I am?"

"I saw you with this woman. Her, I haven't been able to identify, but you popped up in my database. Genius former scientist with DARPA."

"Well, I know who you are," River said. "An arms-dealing prick and a murderer."

Alton leaned forward, and his face—which looked like it had undergone a little too much plastic surgery— took on a hard edge. "Have we danced somewhere before? Are you after the orb for revenge?"

"No," she spat. "But you killed someone I cared about."

Alton shrugged. "I've killed a lot of people. Sometimes sacrifice is necessary."

River growled.

The casino owner dismissed her, focusing on Ty. "I know you want the orb, Dr. Sampson."

Ty remained silent.

"We've been stuck down here since yesterday." Alton raised his gun. "Now, find me the orb."

Ty shook his head. "That's not happening."

Alton stepped forward. "I want it. I *will* be a genius." As he spoke, his eyes widened, his tone filled with fervent belief.

Shit, the guy was unhinged.

"I will change the world," the casino owner continued.

"What you'll get is a prison cell," Ty said.

Suddenly, Alton fired.

The bullet pinged off the wall behind Ty and River.

River dove, knocking into Ty. They ducked down behind a Mercedes. River pulled out her SIG and fired back.

More gunfire broke out.

Cool as a cucumber, she popped up, aiming over the hood, and fired again.

Ty pulled his own SIG and heard one of Alton's goons shout out.

"Hit him," she muttered. "Nothing vital."

Ty pressed his back to the car, brain ticking over. They needed a plan, because right now, they were stuck underground with a crazed billionaire with no way out.

THEY NEEDED to take these bastards down fast.

River heard movement—clothing sliding against metal. She spun around, swinging her weapon with her. She saw one of Alton's guards slip around one of the other cars.

Before she could take a shot, Ty exploded into action. He charged the man, kicking the gun out of his hand. Then he dived on the guard, wrestling him to the ground.

Wow, Ty could fight. She watched him land a wicked punch to the man's head. The man groaned and slumped to the floor.

She smiled. Her man was good in a fight.

Her man. A weird, hot-cold sensation filled her belly. She'd process that later.

She spun. She had to find where Alton was. She strained to pick up any sound.

Suddenly, a hand reached out from below the vehicle she was using for cover. Strong fingers gripped her ankle and yanked. She uttered a mental curse as she fell.

River rolled to her side and saw the thug under the car. She kicked at him, heard a curse, and then she rolled away.

When she rose up on her knee, she saw Chadwick Alton standing nearby. He was aiming his gun at Ty.

"Ty!"

At her scream, he spun.

Alton smiled, his hand tightening on his gun.

This wasn't happening. For a second, she was back in that alley, staring at Jack's body. River leaped, jumping in front of Ty.

The sound of the gunshot was deafening.

River felt a sting on her arm. *Ow.* She hit the ground.

"River!" Ty dropped down, moving toward her.

One of the car alarms started going off, earsplitting in the enclosed space.

She looked down and saw blood on her sleeve. It hurt like hell, but she knew it wasn't bad.

Suddenly, Alton grabbed her and yanked her up. Holding her like a shield, he pressed his gun to her temple.

River froze. She saw Ty do the same, staring at them intently.

She stayed calm. She just had to wait for the right moment. Alton was older, less fit, and upset. She had the advantage. She pulled in a deep, stabilizing breath. Jack had taught her that: stay calm, catalogue your opponent's weaknesses.

"Put down your weapon, Dr. Sampson," Alton ordered.

No. If Ty put his weapon down, he'd leave himself vulnerable. "Ty, don't—"

Ty crouched and set his SIG on the polished concrete floor.

Damn. Him. She pressed her lips together.

The two thugs rushed up to him. The first hit him hard in the face, and then they shoved him against one of the cars.

River bit her tongue. *Don't give Alton any reaction.* When the guards spun Ty around, both of them clutching his arms behind his back, his gaze ran over River.

"She's bleeding," Ty said.

"She'll live," Alton snapped.

River caught Ty's gaze, trying to tell him wordlessly that she was fine.

"I want you to find me the orb, Dr. Sampson."

Ty shook his head. "I don't know—"

Alton jabbed the gun harder into her temple, and she winced.

Ty's gaze zeroed in on her face. Then he looked around, scanning the underground area. "You believe it's down here?"

"We searched the house. It wasn't upstairs."

She could see Ty's mind turning over. He was thinking through the problem, trying to find a way for them to get out of the situation. He was so sexy to watch.

At that moment, River realized she was falling for him. Her chest tightened. Despite knowing better, she'd slipped off the edge, and was tumbling. She licked her lips.

Okay, so she'd worry about falling in love, later. First, they had to get out of here alive.

Ty's attention had moved to the back wall.

Frowning, River did the same. It was just bare concrete, nothing else.

He walked forward. "It's like the wine cellar. The dimensions are off compared to the floor above."

He strode over to the wall and Alton jerked her forward. The guards followed.

Ty reached out, running his hands over the concrete. It looked solid to River. He moved his gorgeous hands over the wall, almost like a caress. Then he turned, frowning as he studied a single groove in the wall where two sheets of concrete met.

Then, he ran his fingers along the groove. A chime sounded and everyone froze.

The entire wall went from solid gray to clear glass in a flash.

River gasped. Alton sucked in a breath.

Beyond the glass was an art gallery. It was packed full of paintings, sculptures, bronzes, and display cabinets filled with smaller objects.

And in the center of the space, resting on a pedestal, was the da Vinci orb.

CHAPTER SIXTEEN

With his face still throbbing, Ty worked quickly to hack into the electronic lock on the door to the gallery. He was amazed that this entire wall was made of electrically switchable smart glass. He'd seen it before, where applying a voltage could change glass from clear to opaque. This glass was even more high-tech—looking exactly like concrete prior to the switch.

The lock beeped and the glass doors whispered open.

Alton shoved his way through, his thugs following.

Ty reached out and grabbed River's hand. He squeezed her fingers.

Her face was impassive and composed. Together, they turned to face the art gallery. *Jesus*. The place was packed to the gills, and he could see plenty of recognizable artwork that he bet cost more than even his father earned in a year.

Alton made a beeline straight to the pedestal with the

orb. The casino owner circled around the sphere, his face lit with a fanatical look.

"This," he said. "This is what I've worked for. I'll change the world."

River rolled her eyes. "Jesus, you sound like a cheesy villain out of a bad B-grade movie."

He shot her a venomous look over his shoulder. "Tie them up."

The guards wasted no time. They shoved Ty and River to the ground, back to back. Then the men bound their hands together with sturdy ropes. They yanked them tight, and Ty fought a wince.

Ty watched as Alton lifted the orb off the pedestal. He held it up in front of him, his expression turning reverent.

"Da Vinci's masterpiece. The elixir of genius."

They needed a plan. *Fast.* Ty tried to work out how much time had passed since they'd been down here. Lachlan and the team would be trying to find them.

"How does it open?" Alton frowned, giving the orb a light shake.

His guards moved closer.

That was when Ty felt River's fingers moving, working on the knots on the ropes. He smiled. That was his wily woman.

He tried to help, but his fingers were going numb. The assholes had tied his rope too tight. But he could help by distracting Alton so they didn't notice what River was doing.

"So, what's your grand plan, Alton?" Ty said. "Wreak havoc, be an asshole?"

"Arsehole," River muttered.

Alton turned, the orb resting on his palm, almost in the same pose as Christ in the *Salvator Mundi*.

"I have a vision," Alton drawled. "I will achieve greatness for the world. It's time for us to transform. To gain strength and eradicate weakness."

"Survival of the fittest." Ty shook his head. "Or survival of the people you deem the strongest, you mean."

Alton frowned. "Why would we want the weak to survive?"

"Everyone has something to offer, Alton. Everyone views strengths differently." He knew this better than anyone. His parents believed his skills nothing more than tinkering. All the members of Team 52 had suffered the end of their regular military careers, usually with a loss of a limb or other trauma, but they were the strongest men and women he knew. "Strength should also be measured by looking beyond the surface, thinking outside the box, and by how we look out for those who are most vulnerable."

Alton snorted. "Strength is about getting to the top." He held up the orb. "It is genius and talent. And if I have to burn the world to ashes to allow a better world to rise up, like a phoenix, then so be it."

A chill went down Ty's spine, and he felt River's fingers falter.

Alton hadn't finished. "Did you know that during the world wars, industry and innovation thrived? People worked harder and came together for a common cause. They invented new things. Countries and allies joined forces to fight back."

"*Against* people who wanted to do what you're doing," River bit out.

Ty sucked in a breath. "You want to start another world war?"

Alton smiled and nodded. "Exactly. And thanks to this—" he gestured to the orb "—I'll be the one to usher in the new ideas and technology the world will need."

Ty felt the rope fall away from River's hands. She was free.

"You're a crazy fuck," River said.

"My team will stop you," Ty said. "That's what they do."

"No one will stop me," Alton returned.

"Wrong." River charged upward, aiming for the closest guard.

RIVER SMASHED into the first thug. Her elbow rammed into his throat and he dropped with a grunt. She whirled and kicked the second guard in the gut. He flew back and hit a cabinet, slumping to the ground.

She spun.

Alton fired his weapon and she ducked. She quickly crouched down and snatched up one of the groaning guards' Glocks.

She raised the gun, striding forward as she fired. *Bang. Bang. Bang.*

But Alton was already diving for cover.

She strode over to the statue where he'd disappeared. No sign of him. Turning slowly, she scanned around.

"River!" Ty yelled.

She swiveled and she saw Alton rushing at her, his face contorted. He held the orb raised above his head.

She braced herself and they slammed together. The orb flew into the air.

"No!" Alton screamed.

Shit. River shoved him away and dived. She caught the orb in her palm, right before she slammed belly-first onto the floor.

Oof. The air rushed out of her. Pulling the orb close, she rolled, whipping up her other hand with the Glock.

She saw Alton scramble behind a display cabinet.

Bloody hell. River pulled in some breaths. She rolled onto her hands and knees, then crawled toward Ty.

"Nice catch," he said.

She reached for the rope still binding his hands behind his back.

Then a gunshot echoed through the gallery.

She glanced back, firing in Alton's direction.

The rope around Ty's wrists was too tight. She cursed, tugging at it. His damn fingers were turning purple.

"Guards have joined Alton," he murmured.

Come on. "They're over there, scheming."

"Our priority is the orb," Ty said.

"Shut up."

"Get the orb out, River. Secure it, get to safety, and find my team. Then come back for me."

Her heart hammered hard in her chest. "They'll kill you."

Dark eyes met hers. "I'll hold them off until you get back."

Dammit. She shook her head, torn. Usually on a mission, she was laser-focused on her objective. The orb felt like it weighed a ton in her hands, and she knew she couldn't let Alton get his hands on it.

Her gut churned. She couldn't leave Ty.

"Ty—"

"Go, River. Your safety is more important to me than that fucking orb, but protecting it is important too. Lock the doors behind you."

She shook her head, yanking on the ropes again. "No. We're both getting out."

Another gunshot rang out, hitting the wall above their heads.

"Go," he said in a stern voice.

She leaned in and kissed him on the lips—hard and fast. Her pulse pounded loudly in her ears. "Don't die, or I'll hunt you down in the afterlife, and I'll kick your ass."

He smiled. "Don't you mean arse?"

Tearing herself away, she bent double, and raced for the door.

She heard shouts and more gunshots.

She reached the door, and jammed her fist against the lock. Once she was on the other side, she watched the doors close. Then she aimed at the locking panel and fired on it.

All the lights on the door controls flickered and died.

Alton reached the other side, shouting as he hammered his fists against the door.

Then he raised his weapon, firing on the glass.

But she'd already deduced the thick glass was bullet-proof. Several starburst cracks appeared, but that was it.

Alton let out a furious cry.

Then she looked past the crazed casino owner and saw Ty sitting there, his handsome face turned her way.

He nodded at her.

Nausea rising in her throat, River turned and ran.

But every step hurt.

CHAPTER SEVENTEEN

Ty listened to Alton rage.

The man was screaming, spittle flying from his mouth. Even his guards were starting to look uncomfortable.

Alton kicked one of the priceless statues and it fell, shattering on the polished-concrete floor. Then he turned and punched a painting, his fist tearing through the canvas.

The casino owner turned, his furious eyes narrowing on Ty. "You won't stop me."

Ty lifted a shoulder. "We already have."

Alton strode forward and Ty braced. The man kicked him, his boot hitting Ty's ribs. He grunted.

Alton stepped back, chest heaving. "Untie him and bring him over here."

The thugs yanked Ty to his feet, and he felt a knife slice through the ropes. Pins and needles flooded his hands. The guards shoved him toward Alton.

Ty kept calm, waiting for a chance so he could grab a gun off one of the guards.

"I'll find her and kill her," Alton said.

Ty smiled. "No, you won't. She's too smart for you."

"Put his hand on the pedestal and hold it flat," Alton ordered.

His men obeyed, flanking Ty and gripping his arms. He struggled, but the two of them were just as big as he was. After a brief scuffle, they managed to slam left his hand flat against the pedestal.

Alton swiveled his gun around, then slammed the butt down on one of Ty's fingers.

He heard the bone break and pain rocketed up his arm.

He bit his tongue, tasting blood. *Fuck.*

"I'll put a bullet in her brain," Alton said.

"She's already beaten you," Ty said. "She's long gone, asshole."

With a choked noise, Alton slammed the gun butt down again and broke another of Ty's fingers.

Ty groaned, biting down to hold back a shout of pain. He didn't want to give Alton the pleasure.

The casino owner grinned. *Sadistic bastard.*

"The orb's gone." Ty rubbed it in. "It's out of reach. My team and my woman will dismantle you, one piece at a time."

The gun butt came down again with another brutal hit.

This time, Ty couldn't hold back his agonized shout. It echoed through the art gallery.

RUMMAGING AROUND in the storage closet, River pulled out a backpack. She tipped out some of the hiking gear that was inside.

She'd already been up the stairs and tried the door back into the kitchen. No luck. She couldn't get the damn thing open.

She shoved some things into the pack.

Then she heard a man's pained roar.

A stone lodged in her throat. *Ty.*

Crouching behind a car, she moved closer. Through the glass, she saw Alton slam his gun butt down onto Ty's hand. Her body jerked.

No. The bastard. Not Ty's hands. Not his beautiful hands.

Fury roared through her like a supernova. She slung the backpack over her shoulder. Anger and fear fueling her, she stormed back through the basement. She wasn't letting Alton hurt Ty. No way in hell.

She climbed into one of the vintage cars—a Ferrari. She yanked the covers off the dash near the steering wheel. She pulled out the wires and set to work hotwiring the car. It was a handy skill Jack had taught her, as he'd bemoaned modern cars and being unable to hotwire them.

Come on. Come on.

A second later, the engine roared to life.

Grim-faced, she gripped the steering wheel and put her foot down. The engine revved.

Then with a squeal of tires, the car leaped forward. She aimed right at the art gallery.

She smashed into the glass wall, and it shattered in a shower of deadly shards.

She crashed into one guard, and he went flying through the air. The other tried to dodge out of the way, but she clipped him and he disappeared under the car.

Ty and Alton dived out of the way.

The car hit the opposite wall with a crunch of metal.

River was jerked around in her seat, but once she was steady, she flung the door open. She marched toward the cowering Alton and kicked him.

Her boot caught his jaw.

"Bitch." He spat out a mouthful of blood.

"Yep." She yanked off the backpack and held it up. "You should never have hurt him."

The casino owner's eyes locked on the round bulge in the backpack.

Then River turned and smashed the backpack against the car.

There was a sound of crunching glass and then fluid leaked out of the backpack.

"Nooooo!" Alton's eyes turned horrified.

River tossed the backpack to the floor. Alton crawled toward it. He picked it up, cradling it like a baby.

She turned and ran to Ty.

He was sitting against the back wall, sweating and in pain. He held his left hand clutched to his chest.

"Ty." She pulled the bandanna from around her neck and quickly reached for his hand. "God." His fingers were a smashed, bloody mess.

Gently, she wrapped the fabric around them. Heat pricked her eyes. These were his tools, what he used to create amazing things.

"I'm alive, River." His voice was tight with pain. "That's all I care about."

Fighting back her emotions, she quickly kissed him.

"You ruined everything!"

Alton's words rang through the room and she quickly turned around.

He stood there now, cold and composed. He was holding a gun aimed at them.

Shit. Anger spurted through her. She'd thought of nothing but getting to Ty, and subsequently forgotten her training. She held up her hands.

Alton jerked the gun. "Let's go."

She rose. "Where—?"

"I don't know," he roared. "But I know his fucking team is out there." He glared at Ty. "I need you two to be my insurance, so I can get out of here."

Ty started to rise, and River slid an arm around him to help.

Alton waved his gun again. "Move it."

Together, the three of them walked out of the gallery, glass crunching beneath their boots. They moved past the cars.

"There's nowhere to go," River said.

Alton led them to the far wall. He raised the gun and fired on the access panel. "Work wasn't a fool. There's an emergency exit."

Suddenly, a secret door clicked open. Behind it, a set of stairs led upward.

"How did you know?" River asked.

"I tortured the house's architect." Alton smiled, his teeth smeared with blood. "He told me lots of interesting things."

"So why didn't you leave?" she said.

His smile went flat. "I wasn't leaving without the orb." Something ugly crossed his face. "But you ruined that. Now, go."

CHAPTER EIGHTEEN

Ty tried to block the pain from his hand. It was a mass of throbbing agony. Their footsteps thumped up the stairs.

"I told you to go," he whispered furiously to River.

"I went. I came back."

"You came back," he repeated.

She looked at him. "Yeah. I can't seem to stay away from you."

Damn. Her words hit him deep inside. This was the worst possible time for him to realize that he was in love with this prickly, dangerous woman.

A door loomed ahead, and River pressed her hands against the emergency bar to open it.

They stumbled outside into a courtyard oasis, blinking in the bright, afternoon sunshine. There were plants growing everywhere, in garden beds and large pots. One entire wall of the courtyard was a vertical garden of lush greenery. The light gleamed off a large pond in the center of the space, a water feature tinkling happily.

Ty looked up. The house wrapped around this courtyard and he studied the windows. He didn't spot any movement, but Lachlan and the others *had* to be in the house.

They had to be close. *Come on, guys.*

He wanted Alton stopped, and River safe.

River's body tensed next to him. She was getting ready to attack Alton. Ty pulled in a breath. Dammit, he wanted her alive, with no bullet holes in her beautiful body.

Alton glanced around, scowling. He pulled a phone out of his pocket and tapped the screen. A chime sounded and Ty arched his neck to see it.

Shit. The man had activated some sort of tracker.

"What now?" River asked.

"We wait." Then Alton looked at the backpack still clutched in his hand. "It wasn't supposed to end like this," he bit out. "With the orb destroyed."

River lifted a shoulder. "Life is full of disappointments."

"Shut up!" He fired the gun at the pond, setting the water rippling.

Ty moved closer to River, pressing his mouth to her ear. "Let's not piss off the unhinged man with the gun."

Alton seemed to find some control. "Both of you get on your knees."

"No," Ty said.

"Do it!" He fired again, the sound reverberating around the courtyard.

He was unraveling. Fast.

A roar of sound overhead made Ty's heart thump against his ribs. He looked up and his stomach dropped.

A black helicopter hovered above them. He saw several black lines drop down, then black-clad mercenaries rappelled over the side of the helo.

Shit. It wasn't his team.

A wide smile crossed Chadwick Alton's face. "Now, get on your knees."

They'd run out of options. He saw the boots of the first armed mercenary hit the tiled courtyard. Ty grabbed River's arm and tugged her down. They dropped to their knees.

She gripped his right hand. "Ty...I..."

He squeezed her fingers hard. "River."

She opened her mouth, then closed it. "I don't want us to die here. I'm not finished with you."

"Good."

Ty spotted another flash of movement from above.

He looked up and this time, his pulse went crazy. He saw several figures in white standing on the rooftop. A second later, they all jumped, CXM rifles clutched in their hands. A whizzing sound filled the air.

Relief flooded him. "You'll be sorry you ever started this, Alton."

Scrambling backward, Alton aimed into the air. "Stop them!"

A gunshot cracked and the gun flew out of Alton's hand. He screamed. His mercenaries swiveled...only to be met with a hail of gunfire.

Team 52 landed all around the courtyard. They were

all using Ty's most recent zipline design. They unclipped the lines from their belts and whipped their weapons up.

The fight was short and brutal. Team 52 easily subdued Alton's men. Weapons clattered to the ground, black-clad bodies jolting and collapsing. Groans filled the air.

"Smith," Lachlan yelled.

The big man aimed his CXM upward. There was a muffled thump, followed by an explosion at the helicopter's windshield. The helicopter veered to the side, a rotor clipping the roof of Laura Work's house.

Ty leaped on River. There was a loud crash, the sound of breaking glass, and the screech of metal.

When he lifted his head, he saw the helo had crashed into the roof. A plume of smoke rose upward.

"What the fuck?" Alton looked around confused and panicked.

Team 52 kicked the weapons away from the wounded mercs. As Axel tied the men up, the others circled around Alton, weapons aimed.

"You two okay?" Lachlan asked.

Ty pressed his bleeding hand to his chest. "We've had better days, but we're okay."

River leaped to her feet, then landed a hard kick to Alton's gut. The casino owner staggered backward and fell into the pond.

Blair smiled. "Nice kick."

Lachlan and Blair both moved to the edge of the pond, rifles aimed directly into Alton's face.

The man came up spitting out water. "No." He shook his soggy hair. "It wasn't supposed to be like this!"

Then he raised a hand out of the water. Ty's gut contracted. The man was holding something.

"Grenade!" Ty shouted.

Alton threw the device.

Ty heard the clunk as it hit the flagstone tiles and bounced. He saw Lachlan and Blair jump into the pond.

Ty leaped on River and they rolled into a garden bed.

Boom.

Debris flew up in the air around them. Their earpieces filled with curses.

Ty sat up. "Okay?"

"Yeah." River nodded, her hair askew. "You?"

"Yes." He cupped her face.

They turned and watched as a wet, pissed-off Lachlan dragged Alton out of the pond.

"Everyone all right?" the Team 52 leader called out.

The rest of the team came out of cover, all of them scowling at Alton.

Ty tugged River closer. "I think I need to tell you now, so you have time to get used to it, that I'm falling in love with you, River Elliott-Hall."

Her eyes widened. "No."

"Yes."

"No."

"Yes," he said firmly.

She looked at her boots. "Shit."

With a laugh, he pulled her close and kissed the side of her head.

Alton, held by the back of the neck by Seth and looking like a drowned, deranged rat glared at River.

"You destroyed the orb. You've condemned us all to weakness and failure!"

"Anyone else think he sounds like a B-grade movie villain?" Axel asked.

Lachlan's head swiveled to River and Ty. "The orb was destroyed?"

River straightened. "Actually, it's stashed in the back seat of an Aston Martin down in the basement."

Silence fell around the courtyard. Alton's mouth dropped open.

Ty raised a brow. "So, what's in the backpack?"

"Some spare lightbulbs and a bottle of water."

Blair smiled. "Nice work, MI6."

River smiled back. "You like me now?"

"Jury's still out, so don't push it," Blair replied.

Ty pulled River close and their noses brushed. "Jury's not still out for me."

Warmth flared in her eyes. "Good."

RIVER SAT IN THE X8, tired and more than a little sore.

They were headed back to Las Vegas. Lachlan and Blair had dealt with the San Francisco police and the pissed-off widow of a tech billionaire. Laura Work had been furious at the invasion of her home, destruction of her art collection, and the confiscation of the Da Vinci orb.

But there wasn't much she could do about it.

While Lachlan had dealt with that headache, River

held a grumpy Ty's good hand as Callie had treated his damaged one. It was now splinted and bandaged, and Callie had bullied him into some painkillers.

The orb was resting in a containment box in the back of the X8.

She was pretty sure she never wanted to see it again.

River leaned into Ty, absorbing his warmth. She'd never leaned before. She'd always felt the need to be strong for her mum, and there would always be a distance between her and her dad. She didn't trust him enough to lean on him.

But Ty Sampson accepted her just as she was—warts and all. Hell, he seemed to like her warts.

She could deal with *like*, but she wasn't even thinking about the other "L" word.

His big hand stroked her hair and she absorbed that small caress. She bit her lip. There was more fear in her belly than when she'd been facing Alton's gun.

Lachlan sat down in the seat across from them. His face had a serious look, as usual.

"You want a job?"

River blinked and felt Ty stiffen beside her. "With Team 52?"

Lachlan's lips quirked. "No, with Distinction Cleaning. Yes, with Team 52."

"Well..." For the first time in her life, River felt flustered. "I didn't know you were hiring."

Ty squeezed her hand, and that steadied her.

"We're not hiring just anyone."

"I'm not really a team player," she said.

"Could have fooled me," Lachlan replied. "You

worked well with us, and you have skills. We could use someone like you." Lachlan's golden gaze flicked to Ty, then back. "Think about it."

Lachlan rose and moved back to sit with Axel, Callie, and Smith.

River swallowed. She had a life in London. She couldn't just join a black ops team in the US. Could she? Panic fluttered in her chest.

When she looked up, she saw Ty's dark gaze was on her face. "You going to disappear?"

"Maybe." Her heart clenched into a tight ball.

"Don't."

That single word reverberated through her soul. "Why?"

"Because I love you."

Her throat went thick. "We're too sensible for that, Ty. We don't believe in fairytales."

"Nope." He leaned in close. "But I believe in living my life. I believe in reality, which is you and me." He smiled. "Besides, you love me, too."

Her eyebrows winged up. "You're insane."

He kissed her. A teasing brush, then his mouth closed over hers. His tongue stroked hers, deepening the kiss. She wound an arm around his neck and kissed him back.

"Get a room," Axel called out.

Ty took his time finishing the kiss. He kept one arm wrapped around her, holding her close.

River just let her mind go blank and held on.

Soon, they swept in to land at Area 52. The base was lit up brightly. When they stepped off the X8, she watched Ty slip into work mode. The grumpy, serious scientist was back again. She watched him barking out orders as guards whisked the orb containment box off to his lab.

She watched him walk into the hangar, her gaze on his magnificent ass. So handsome. And he loved *her*.

She could hardly believe it.

Blair stepped up beside her, the woman's shoulder brushing River's. "The jury's not still out, MI6. The way you look at him..." Blair nodded, her blonde ponytail bouncing. "You'll do, Elliott-Hall." Blair slapped her on the shoulder. "But I won't go easy on you in training."

"Never asked you to." *If* River joined the team. She flashed a grin at the other woman, who nodded and made her way inside.

As the group moved inside the hangar, River looked around. She could make a place for herself here.

All she had to do was trust and take a leap.

She pulled in a deep breath. She'd let herself think it over. The first thing she had to do was finish her job. She needed to call the museum and get the *Salvator Mundi* back where it belonged.

Then, she'd decide what to do about the rest of her life.

CHAPTER NINETEEN

Ty was back in his lab. He had da Vinci's orb resting on a stand on the bench and he was running tests.

He was also grumpy and distracted. He wasn't having much luck with his investigation of the orb, and he hadn't seen River for several hours today.

He blew out a breath. But his biggest problem was that he had no idea if she'd stay.

She'd slept wrapped around him last night, but he still wasn't sure what she'd decide. He ran a hand over his head. He had no idea if his love—which was rusty at best —was enough incentive for her to give up her entire life.

Pressing his hands to the bench, careful not to put too much weight on his healing fingers, he dropped his head forward. He couldn't force her to stay. He couldn't force her to love him.

Trust him not to fall in love with some easy, sweet woman. He snorted. Right. An easy woman would put up with him for about three seconds.

Trying hard to focus on his work, he picked up his tablet, careful of his bandaged hand. He'd X-rayed it himself, and thankfully, the breaks would all heal. He saw the new results on the fluid in the orb were in. He frowned. *Dammit.* Right now, everything was saying it was simply water.

He sat down heavily on a stool and set the tablet down. He'd run some extra tests. He wasn't going to let da Vinci beat him.

Suddenly, his hands were jerked behind his back, and a rope slithered around his wrists. The rope tightened.

"What the fuck?"

"Gotcha," River drawled from behind him.

Her voice made him go still. He looked back over his shoulder. She was tying his arms together.

"River—"

She pressed in close to his side, nipping at his earlobe. Her fingers brushed over his bandaged hand gently. "It's been way too long without you."

He made a humming sound.

She slithered around, climbing into his lap. "You've made me addicted to you, Ty."

She kissed him, and he kissed her back eagerly. "I'm not sorry."

With a smile, she ground down against him, and his cock went hard.

"Have you ever done it in your lab?"

"No." His brain was bombarded with sexy images of River, stretched out naked among his experiments.

"I locked the door on the way in." Her smile turned

feline. "And your team are all catching up on some sleep."

"There are cameras—"

"Pfft." She waved a hand. "I shut them down."

"When Brooks realizes, he'll have a meltdown."

"Then he'd better come up with some better way to secure his system." River slid off the stool and dropped down between Ty's legs. Her fingers worked his belt.

He groaned. "River."

With expert hands, she freed his cock. She made a hungry, little, humming sound, then leaned forward and used her mouth.

Ty groaned, his gaze moving to the ceiling. He thrust his hips forward, his gaze dropping to the mind-blowing sight of River's lips wrapped around his cock. He thrust his hips again to push more of his cock into her sweet mouth.

"I want to be inside you," he growled. "I want to come inside you."

With a loud pop, she slipped her mouth off his cock and stood. She shimmied out of her clothes and stood naked in front of him. So damn gorgeous.

Then she straddled him. He saw her hold up a small foil square. She tore it open and as she slid the condom over his cock, he bit his lip to hold in his groan. Then, using his shoulders for leverage, she lined his cock up between her legs. She slowly lowered herself down.

Ty jerked against the bindings, wishing he could hold her, but a part of him liked the feeling of being restrained. Of her using him and taking what she wanted.

He watched her face. *God, her face.* When they'd first

met, she'd been so enigmatic, so closed off. Now, she showed him everything.

She rode him slowly. It was both torture and joy, pleasure and pain. She looked into his eyes, panting. Their breath mingled.

"You're mine," he growled. "Admit it."

She shook her head. "No, you're *mine*."

"You joining the team?"

She slid down again, taking him deep inside her. "I already did."

They both groaned now. River started to move faster, slamming her hips against him.

"Do you love me?" he asked.

"I love your cock. I love your goatee, your sexy lips, your gorgeous body, your brain. So yeah, I guess I do love you."

Elation roared through him. With a few quick flicks of his fingers, he untied the rope. As he wrapped his arms around her, her chin jerked up.

"Hey."

"You taught me how to escape."

He slid his uninjured hand beneath her ass and rose. He set her on the bench and leaned forward, hammering hard inside her.

"Oh. God." Her head fell back. "Yes."

He'd never get enough of her. The tight clasp of her body drove him toward the edge. Ty never wanted to get enough of her.

"Ty, I'm going to come."

"Come."

A second later, they both cried out and found release together.

———

RIVER HAD JUST FINISHED her first training session with Team 52. She was tired, sweaty, and happy.

"Ms. Elliott-Hall," one of the Air Force guards called out to her as she walked back into the Area 52 hangar. "There are some people here to see you."

She nodded. "Thanks."

Once her eyes adjusted to the gloom inside, she spotted Jonah talking with two men. Today, the director was wearing a tailored, deep-blue suit. He was talking with two dark-haired, brown-skinned men. One wore a suit, and the other the traditional Emirati clothing of a long, loose-fitting kandura robe, with a red-and-white-checked headdress.

She walked toward them and the man in the kandura stepped forward. "Hello, Ms. Elliott-Hall. A pleasure to see you again."

River inclined her head. "Prince Abdullah."

"Director Grayson informs me that you have the *Salvator Mundi* ready for transport."

She nodded.

"Everyone at the Louvre Abu Dhabi thanks you for your excellent work. Payment has been transferred to your account."

"Thank you."

"No, thank *you*. Our country has invested a lot of

money into the *Salvator Mundi*. Its loss would have been immense."

As the two men from the Louvre moved off with some guards to collect the painting, Jonah gave her a faint smile and stalked off. River headed toward the elevator down to the Area 52 base. She needed a shower.

Her final freelance job was complete, and she was now officially a member of Team 52. Jonah had carved the visa red tape like a samurai sword through a feather. Sometimes it paid to be black ops. She still had to head back to London, sort out her apartment, and tell her father she was leaving. But when she got back to Las Vegas, she was moving in with Ty.

She paused, looking out the hangar doors to the desert. In just days, her life had changed completely. At times, it still didn't even feel real.

Suddenly, a hard blow hit her in the back.

River stumbled forward and spun, moving into a fighting stance. Blair stood behind her, bouncing on the balls of her feet, grinning. The blonde waggled her fingers.

With a grin, River darted forward.

They traded blows, moving across the hangar. Right away, she was well aware they were gaining an audience. She blocked a kick and then came up with a punch.

Blair spun, and landed a blow to River's back, sending her stumbling forward. A hard punch hit River's nose. She cursed, then crouched and came up fast, landing a punch to Blair's jaw. The woman's head snapped back.

Then Blair dived, tackling River to the ground. They

rolled across the concrete floor, each trying to pin the other.

They were evenly matched.

Blair started laughing. "Yeah, you'll do, Elliott-Hall."

They rolled off each other, kneeling on the ground. "You almost broke my nose."

"Then move faster next time. And don't break Ty's heart."

"I love him." River shoved her hair back. God, she loved the man so much it was crazy.

"Why do you sound so shocked?" Blair asked.

"Because I am." She was still afraid. Afraid she'd mess this up. Afraid he'd wake up one day and decide she wasn't worth it.

"I was the same with MacKade." Blair gave a happy sigh. "I wouldn't change a thing. Anything worth having is risky, you just have to fight for it."

A smile tugged at River's lips. "I'm good at fighting."

"I know."

Both women pushed to their feet. "We having a heart-to-heart, Mason?"

"Hell, no."

Elbowing each other, they headed for the elevator.

River went to her newly assigned quarters at the base. She quickly showered and changed, then headed to Ty's lab.

Halfway down the corridor, Arlo appeared. He scanned her before his pale blue eyes met hers. "Heard you joined the team, MI6?"

"I did."

He nodded. "And heard you kicked ass on the mission in San Francisco."

She smiled. "I always kick arse, Arlo."

"Arse?" He shook his head. "Gonna have to get you talking right."

"I speak the Queen's English, so that means you're the one who's not speaking correctly."

His eyes crinkled. "You have sass. I like it." He tilted his head. "And you somehow softened up Sampson."

River winked. "That man is not soft, I promise you."

That earned her a gruff laugh. "Get out of here."

She waved jauntily over her shoulder as she continued down the hall. When she pushed the lab door open, thoughts of Arlo evaporated. Instead, her head filled with memories of the sexy times she and Ty had shared in there the day before. *Mmm.*

Ty looked up and smiled at her. He looked very pleased with himself.

"Either you just had some nookie...which means I'd have to kill you. Or you worked it out."

He pulled her close and smacked a kiss to her lips. "I worked it out. I know how da Vinci's elixir works."

Seconds later, the door opened and the rest of the team barged inside, filling the lab. Smith, Lachlan, and Seth leaned against the wall. Axel sat on a stool, while Blair and Callie pulled themselves up on the benches. Nat and Brooks stood nearby. Jonah was the last to arrive, nodding at Ty.

"The drug stimulates nerve growth in the brain," Ty said. "We all know that when you create a new habit, it forms new neurons in your brain and helps make that action easier over time. Da Vinci's fluid accelerates that process so it's nearly instantaneous."

Wow. River looked at the orb and the fluid inside.

"But there are downsides." Ty's face turned even more serious than usual. "It can have some other effects on the brain which aren't so pleasant. It decreases a person's social skills, and also decreases concentration. It makes people more unfocused."

Nat leaned forward. "Da Vinci was notorious for never finishing things. He'd start a job, but never get to the end."

"And Sam Work was known to be arrogant, unfriendly, and difficult to work with," Brooks said.

Jonah tapped a finger against his jaw. "Run more tests, Ty. I want to know if it's safe to use it sparingly, and in the right situations."

"Will do."

With a nod, the director headed off. Callie leaped off the bench. "The X8 is heading back to Vegas soon. Who's up for a night at Griffin's?" She smiled at River. "We need to welcome River to the team."

There were cheers and agreement all around.

Soon, they were all packed onto the X8, heading back in to the city.

"We'll head to Griffin's for a quick drink." Ty nuzzled River's neck. "Then I want to get home."

She rolled her eyes at him. "God, we're an old, married couple already."

"Yep."

It wasn't long before the team was all seated at Griffin's. Blair and Axel were locked in a battle at the pool table. Everyone's significant other had arrived. MacKade was chatting with Lachlan, who had his arm slung around Rowan. Seth was standing behind January, his palms resting over the mound of her pregnant belly. Kinsey was nestled in Smith's lap as they sat at the bar. Nat and Callie were sharing a bottle of white wine.

River sipped her drink. Somehow, she'd ended up with all these new friends. A family, of sorts. She stared at Ty. And love.

She knew Jack would be happy. Her mum, too.

"Where's Brooks?" she asked.

Ty sipped his beer. "Picking up some fancy computer part that he'd ordered. He's been drooling about it arriving."

"Speaking of new things, I have a surprise for you," she said.

His dark brows rose. "Oh?"

She leaned in close. "I picked up some nice, new silk ropes for us to test out at home."

Ty slid an arm along her shoulders and laughed. "Life won't ever be dull with you around, River."

"Never."

CHAPTER TWENTY

Brooks

B rooks stepped into his favorite Las Vegas computer store. It was packed with parts and equipment. He always loved coming in here.

"Eamon, my man," Brooks called out.

"Brooks." The store owner, the same age as Brooks, stepped out from behind the counter. He wore a pair of coke-bottle glasses and a wide smile.

While Brooks had never been the stereotypical geek —he'd loved sports and people too much—Eamon looked every part the cliché nerd. He wore a sweater-vest over his shirt, was round at the waist, and already had a bald spot. But the man had made a killing from his chain of computer stores, so he no longer lived at home with his parents. Last Brooks had heard, he now lived with a tall, well-endowed former showgirl who was head over heels for him.

Eamon's eyes lit up. "I got it."

Excited, Brooks watched his friend set a box down on the counter. Brooks flipped it open and saw the part he'd been waiting for. Rare and expensive as hell, it was just what he wanted.

"It took a lot to find it," Eamon said.

"Great work, buddy."

"What are you planning to do with it?"

Brooks winked. "Top-secret."

"Well, enjoy."

"I'll transfer payment today." Brooks picked up the box.

"I know you're good for it. Tell me how it works out."

Brooks exited the store. He was late to meet the team at Griffin's. Everyone wanted to celebrate a job well done and officially welcome River to the team.

Hell, Ty—of all people—had fallen in love. Brooks shook his head. The love bug was definitely going around.

Setting off down the sidewalk, Brooks shifted his shoulders. He wanted to meet someone too. In fact, he wanted the whole package when it came to a woman—sexy, smart, caring. He sighed. Unfortunately, he always seemed to attract the wrong types. It didn't help that he worked with some of the best women out there—smart, brave, gorgeous.

And way out of his league.

He saw two big guys approaching ahead on the sidewalk and moved to the side to let them pass. He was contemplating how much money he'd lose to Blair at the pool table, when the back of his neck prickled.

The two burly, neckless guys were watching him.

The muscles along Brooks' shoulders tensed.

Something made him glance back over his shoulder. Two more men were moving in behind him.

Fuck.

He quickly darted left, crossing the street.

The four men broke into a jog, coming after him.

Brooks hustled and launched into a sprint. He'd barely reached the other curb when gunfire broke out behind him.

Shit. He hit the ground, the box with his new part crushed beneath him. He leaped up and ran, dodging between two parked cars.

He kept running, and heard footsteps coming in fast behind him. Ahead, he spotted a small park, just starting to turn green again after the winter. He swiveled, running into it. As he pounded down the path, he dodged some teenagers on skateboards. He reached into his pocket, found his electronic fob, and pressed down on the alert button.

Circling some trees, he leaped over a park bench, and came back out on another street. If he could just get to where he'd parked his truck, he'd be home free.

A heavy force slammed into his legs, tackling him from behind. His box flew out of his hand.

Hitting the ground with a grunt, Brooks rolled, already pulling his fist back. He landed a hard punch to his attacker's face.

"Fuck!" the man exploded.

Brooks didn't spend all of his time in his computer

room. He worked out daily, and trained with Team 52. He wasn't afraid of a fight.

He slammed the guy in the head again, kicking his legs. Another punch, and the guy's eyes rolled back in his head.

Yeah, he'd been expecting a tech geek.

Brooks shoved the guy off him, and leaped to his feet.

Two more men rushed at him. As one swung out an arm, Brooks landed a hard front kick into the man's gut. He flew backward.

You picked the wrong guy to tangle with, assholes. As the second man moved, Brooks launched into a roundhouse kick. The guy fell like he'd hit a wall.

Another guy stepped back, looking wary.

Suddenly, something pinched Brooks' chest. An electric shock ran over him, and his teeth clashed together. The pain was agonizing. *Fuck.*

He looked down to see the prongs of a Taser attached to the front of his shirt.

Fuck. Fuck.

Then his legs gave out and he dropped to the concrete, his body twitching.

Darkness swallowed him whole.

TY SET his empty beer bottle down. He was ready to head home.

Suddenly, everyone's phones beeped, including his.

"Shit." Axel groaned. "It's our night off."

Lachlan's brows drew together and he glanced at his phone. "Brooks activated his alert."

Everyone straightened. Ty frowned at the screen of his phone, seeing the emergency alert.

"Could it be a false alarm?" River asked.

"He's tripped it before, when he'd been doing some testing," Ty said.

Callie frowned. "He didn't have any testing planned today."

Blair tapped on her phone and lifted it to her ear. "He's not answering."

Ty tapped on his phone screen. "I'm pulling up his phone tracker." A red dot appeared. "His phone isn't moving. He's downtown."

"That's where the computer shop is," Callie said.

Lachlan stood. "We'll go and check it out."

"Wait," Blair said. "He just texted. *Sorry, guys. False alarm.*"

Everyone relaxed.

"Tell him that he's buying the next round when he gets here," Ty said.

"He says he can't make it." Blair shook her head, smiling. "He has a date with his fancy, new computer part."

"Geek," Axel said good-naturedly.

Callie was still frowning. "It's not like him to pass on drinks, though. He was excited to come, after being stuck at base during the mission."

"The lure of the computer part is strong." Blair eyed River. "MI6, you play pool?"

Ty watched an evil smile spread over his woman's face. "You're on, Mason."

"This should be fun," MacKade drawled.

As River sauntered to the pool table, Ty watched the sexy sway of her ass.

"You've got it bad, *mi amigo*," Axel drawled.

Ty didn't even glance at his friend. "Yep."

"I'm happy for you. Although, your woman is dangerous. Just be careful you don't piss her off and find yourself drugged and tied up."

Ty smiled. "She's very good with a rope."

Axel groaned. "Don't rub your kinky sex life in my face. My sex life is sadly lacking at the moment."

"Why?" Ty raised a brow. "You having a bit of a dry spell?"

Axel shrugged a shoulder. His gaze moved toward the bar, where January, Rowan, and Natalie were sitting. "Something like that."

Ty followed his teammate's gaze and smiled. He slapped Axel firmly on the back. "Time to open your eyes, my friend." Ty rose and headed for the pool table. He wanted to be close enough that his woman didn't get into a fight with Blair.

Callie slipped off her stool. "I'm going to find Brooks and drag his ass here."

As she headed out, everyone raised their hands and wished her luck.

Ty slid his arm around River. "Play nice."

She turned around and kissed his lips. "I never play nice."

Ty smiled to himself, knowing that he had a lifetime ahead of him to play with his dangerous, gorgeous woman.

I hope you enjoyed River and Ty's story!

Team 52 will continue with Brooks' story, *Mission: Her Freedom*. Find out what happens to Team 52's tattooed tech geek later in 2019.

For more action-packed romance, and for a peek at *Treasure Hunter Security* owner Declan Ward's action-packed story, read on for a preview of *Undiscovered*.

Don't miss out! For updates about new releases, action romance info, free books, and other fun stuff, sign up for my VIP mailing list and get your *free box set* containing three action-packed romances.

Visit here to get started: www.annahackettbooks.com

FREE BOX SET DOWNLOAD

JOIN THE ACTION-PACKED ADVENTURE!

PREVIEW: UNDISCOVERED

S he was hot, dusty, and she'd never felt better.

Dr. Layne Rush walked across her dig, her boots sinking into the hot Egyptian sand. Ahead, she saw her team of archeologists and students kneeling over the new section of the dig, dusting sand away with brushes and small spades, methodically uncovering a recently discovered burial ground.

To her left, the yawning hole in the ground where they'd started the dig was like a large mouth, ringed on one side by a wooden scaffold.

In there, below the sands, was a fantastic tomb, and Layne was only beginning to unravel its secrets.

She paused and drew in a breath of warm desert air. To the east lay the Nile, the lifeblood of Egypt. She swiveled and watched the red-orange orb of the sun sinking into the Western Desert sands. All around, the dunes glowed. It made her think of gold.

Excitement was a hit to her bloodstream. Only days ago, they'd discovered some stunning golden artifacts down in the excavation. She'd found the first one—a small ushabti funerary figurine that would have been placed there to serve the tomb's as-yet-unknown occupant in the afterlife. After that, her team had discovered jewelry, a golden scarab, and a small amulet of a dog-like animal.

Stars started appearing in the sky, like tiny pinpricks of light through velvet. She breathed in again. The most exciting thing was the strange inscriptions carved into the dog amulet.

They had mentioned Zerzura.

Oh, Layne really wanted to believe Zerzura existed— a fabulous lost oasis in the desert, filled with treasure. She smiled as she watched the night darkness shroud the dunes. Her parents had read her bedtime stories of Zerzura as a child.

Thoughts of her parents, and the hard punch of grief that followed, made Layne's smile disappear. Unfortunately, life had taught her that fairytales didn't exist.

She shook off the melancholy. She'd made a life for herself, a career, and spent most of her time off on adventures on remote dig sites. She'd held treasures in her hands. She shared her love of history with anyone who'd listen. She hoped that if her mom and dad were still alive, they'd be proud of what she'd achieved.

Layne made her way toward the large square tents set up for dealing with the artifacts. One was for storage and one for study.

"Hey, Dr. Rush."

Layne spotted her assistant, Piper Ross, trudging up the dune toward her. The young woman was smart, opinionated, and not afraid to speak her mind. Her dark hair was cut short, the tips colored purple.

"Hi, Piper."

The young woman grinned. "Give you a whip and you'd look like something out of a movie." Piper swept a palm through the air. "Dr. Rush, dashing female adventurer."

Layne rolled her eyes. "Don't start. I still haven't lived down that last interview I did." What Layne had thought was a serious article on archeology had morphed into a story that turned her into a damned movie character. They'd even Photoshopped a whip in her hand and a hat on her head. "How's that new eastern quadrant coming along?"

"Excellent." Piper stopped, swiping her arm across her sweaty forehead. "I've got it all documented and photographed, and the tape laid out. We're ready to start digging tomorrow morning."

"Well done." Layne was hoping the new area would yield some excellent finds.

"Well, I *am* insanely good at my job—that's why you hired me, remember?" Piper grinned.

Layne tapped her chin. "Was that it? I thought it was

because you kept me in a constant supply of Diet Coke and chocolate."

Piper snorted. "Here they call it Coke Light, remember?"

Layne screwed up her nose. "I remember. The damn stuff doesn't taste the same."

"Yes, you really have to suffer out here on these remote digs."

"Can the sarcasm, Ross. Or I might forget why I keep you around."

Piper laughed. "A few of us are heading into Dakhla for the evening. Want to come?"

Dakhla Oasis was a two-hour drive north-east of the dig site. A group of communities, including the main town of Mut, were centered on the oasis. It was also where most of their local workers came from, and where they got their supplies.

Layne shook her head. "No, but thanks for the offer. I want to spend a bit more time on the artifacts we found, and take another look at the tomb plans. The main burial chamber and sarcophagus have to be in there somewhere."

"Unless grave robbers got to it," Piper suggested.

Layne shook her head. "When that local boy discovered this place it was clearly undisturbed." In between the discovery that had made headlines and her university being awarded the right to dig, the Egyptian Ministry of Antiquities had kept tight security on the place. She knew the Ministry would have preferred to run the dig themselves, but they just didn't have the funding to run every dig in the country. "I'm going to find out who's buried here, Piper."

The younger woman shook her head. "Well, just remember, all work and no play makes Dr. Rush very boring and in need of getting laid."

Layne rolled her eyes. "I'll worry about my personal life, thanks for your concern."

Piper stuck her hand on her hip. "You haven't dated since Dr. Stevens."

Ugh. Just hearing her colleague's name made Layne's stomach turn over. Dr. Evan Stevens had been a colossal mistake. He was tall and handsome, in a clean-cut way that suited his academic career as a professor of the Classics and History.

He'd been nice, intelligent. They'd liked the same restaurants. The sex hadn't been stellar, but it was fine. Layne had honestly thought he was someone she could come to love. More than anything, Layne wanted it all—a career, to travel, a husband who loved her, and most importantly, a family of her own. She wanted the love she remembered her parents sharing. She wanted the career they'd only dreamed of for her.

Maybe that had blinded her to the fact that Evan was an asshole hiding in an expensive suit.

Layne waved a hand dismissively. "I've told you before, I don't want to hear that man's name."

"I know you guys had a bad breakup..."

Ha. Piper didn't know half of it. Evan had stolen some of Layne's research and passed it off as his own. And he'd had the gall to tell her she was bad in bed. Moron.

"Look, go," Layne said. "Head into the oasis, soak in the springs, relax. You've got a lot of work to do tomorrow in the hot sun."

Piper groaned. "Don't remind me."

But Layne could see the twinkle of excitement in the young woman's eye. Layne saw it in her own every day. Being on a dig was always like that. Uncovering a piece of history...she could never truly describe how it made her feel. To touch something that someone had made, used, and cherished thousands of years ago. To uncover its secrets and try to piece together where it fit into the story of the world. To see what they could learn from it that might help them understand more about humanity.

She found it endlessly fascinating. Best job in the world.

After waving Piper off, Layne headed to the storage tent. The canvas door was still rolled up and secured at the top. As she stepped inside, the temperature dropped a little. Now that the sun had set, the temperature would drop even more. Nights in the desert, even in spring, could be chilly. She'd need to get to the portable shower they had set up and rinse off before it got too cold.

She'd lost count of the number of digs she'd been on. In the jungle, in the desert, under cities, by the ocean. She didn't care where they were, she just loved the challenge and thrill of uncovering the past.

Layne flicked on the battery-powered lantern hanging on the side of the tent. Makeshift shelves lined the space. Most were bare, waiting for the treasures they had yet to discover. But the first shelf was lined with shards of pottery, faience amulets, and stone carvings.

But it was the locked box at the base of the shelf she was most interested in.

She quickly dialed in the code on the tumbler-style lock and lifted the lid.

God. She stroked the ushabti reverently, its gold surface glowing in the lantern-light. Her parents would have loved to have seen this. To know their daughter had been the one to find it.

The necklace was still in pieces, but back in their lab in Cairo, someone would piece it back together. The chunky golden scarab would fit perfectly in the palm of her hand. She carefully lifted the small, dog-like amulet. It was slightly smaller than the scarab, and the canine had a slender body like a greyhound, and a long, stiff tail that was forked at the end. She was sure this was a set-animal, the symbol of the Egyptian god, Seth. She stroked the hieroglyphs on the animal's body and the symbols that spelled Zerzura.

Unfortunately, none of the hieroglyphs here made sense. She'd spent hours working on them. They were gibberish.

There was a noise behind her. A scrape of a boot in sand.

She turned, wondering who else had stayed behind.

A fist collided with her face in a vicious blow.

Pain exploded through Layne's cheek and she tasted blood. The blow sent her sprawling into the sand, the set-animal carving falling from her fingers.

Layne couldn't seem to focus. She lay there, her cheek to the sand, trying to clear her head. Her face throbbed and she heard voices talking in Arabic.

A black boot appeared in her line of sight.

A hand reached down and picked up the set-animal.

She swallowed, trying to get her brain working. Then she heard another voice. Deep, cool tones with a clipped British accent that made her blood run cold.

"Move it. I want it done. Fast."

She saw more people come into view. They were all wearing black balaclavas.

They started grabbing the artifacts and stuffing them into canvas bags.

"No." In her head her cry came out loud and outraged. In reality, it was a hoarse whisper.

"Bag everything," the cold voice behind her said.

No. She wasn't letting these thieves steal the artifacts. This was *her* dig and these were her antiquities to safeguard.

She pushed up onto her hands and knees. "Stop." She swung around and kicked at the knee of the man closest to her.

He tipped sideways with a cry.

"Uh-uh." The man with the cold voice stepped into her view. All she saw were his shiny black boots. Before she could do anything else, a hand grabbed her hair and yanked her head back.

The pain made her grit her teeth. Tears stung her eyes. She twisted, trying to pull away from him.

"A spitfire. I do like a feisty woman. Shame I don't have time to play with you."

He was behind her and she couldn't see his face. She tried to jerk away but a hard fist slammed into her head again.

No, no, no. Her vision dimmed, the sound of the thieves' voices receded.

Everything went black.

DECLAN WARD STRODE into the warehouse, his boots echoing on the scarred concrete. Colorado sunlight streamed through the large windows which offered a fantastic view of downtown Denver.

He was gritty-eyed from lack of sleep, and he was still adjusting to being back on Mountain Time.

He'd gotten in from finishing a job in South East Asia sometime around midnight. He'd unlocked his apartment, stumbled in and stripped, and fallen facedown on his bed.

Now, he was headed to work.

Lucky for him, it paid to be one of the owners. He lived above the warehouse that housed the main offices of Treasure Hunter Security.

Most of the open-plan space that had been a flour mill in a previous life was empty. But at the far end it was a different story.

Flat screens covered the brick wall, all displaying different images and scrolling feeds. Some sleek desks were set up, all covered in high-end computers.

There was a small kitchenette tucked into one corner, and next to that sat some sagging couches that looked like they'd come from a charity shop or some college student's house. Just beyond those, near the large windows, were a pool table and an air hockey table.

"Dec? What are you doing here?"

A small, dark-haired woman popped up from her seat at one of the computers. As always, she was dressed stylishly in dark jeans, a soft red sweater the color of raspberries, and impossibly high heels.

"I work here," he said. "Actually, I own the place. Have the mortgage to prove it."

His sister came right up to him and threw her arms around him. He did the same and absorbed the non-stop energy that Darcy always seemed to emit. She'd never been able to sit still, even as a little girl.

"You just got back. You're supposed to have a week off." She patted his arms and frowned. She had the same gray eyes he did, but hers always seemed to look bluer than his.

"Finished the job, ready for the next one."

Her frown deepened, her hands landing on her hips. "You work too hard."

"Darce, I'm tired, and not really up for this rant this morning." She had this spiel down to a fine art.

She huffed out a breath. "Okay. But I'm not done. Expect an earful later."

Great. He tweaked her nose. He'd done it ever since she was a cute little girl in pigtails and dirt-stained clothes tagging around after him and their brother Callum. Dec knew she hated it.

"Hey, Dec. When did you get back?"

Dec clasped hands with one of his team. Hale Carter was a big man, topping Dec's six-foot-two by a couple of inches. He'd been a hell of a soldier, was a bit of a genius with anything mechanical, and a guy who managed to smile through it all. He had a wide smile and dark skin courtesy of his African American mother, and a handsome face that drew the ladies like flies.

But Dec knew the man had secrets too, dark ones. Hell, they all did. They'd all been to some terrible places with the SEAL teams. All had seen and done some things that left scars—both physical and mental.

Dec never pried. He offered jobs to the former soldiers who wanted to work—ones where they normally wouldn't get shot at while doing them—and he didn't ask them to reveal all their demons.

Some demons could never be vanquished. He felt his gut tighten. Dec had accepted that long ago.

"Got in last night. Nice to be home." But even as he said the words, Dec knew it wasn't true. He was already feeling the itch to be out, moving, doing something.

It had been two and a half years since he'd left the Navy and stopped heading into the world's worst war zones. Hell, he didn't leave—they'd booted him out. He'd just barely avoided a dishonorable discharge, but they'd wanted him gone anyway, and he didn't blame them.

He shoved his hands into the pockets of his jeans. In those two and a half years, he'd put together Treasure Hunter Security with his brother and sister, and he'd never looked back. Or at least, he tried not to.

Hale was one of their newest recruits and had fit right in.

Dec made his way to the kitchenette and poured a cup of coffee from the pot. Darcy would have made it, which meant it was barely drinkable, but it was black and strong and had caffeine, so it ticked the boxes.

He saw his best friend slouched on one of the couches, his boots on the scarred coffee table and his long legs cased in well-worn jeans. He was flicking a switchblade open and closed.

"Logan."

"Dec."

Logan O'Connor was another SEAL buddy, and the best friend Dec had ever had. They hadn't liked each other at first, but after a particularly brutal mission—followed by an equally brutal bar fight in the seedy backstreets of Bangkok where they had saved each other's backs—they'd formed a bond.

Logan was big as well, the rolled-up sleeves of his shirt showing off his muscled arms and tattoos. From the day they'd left the military, Logan had let his brown hair grow long and shaggy, and his cheeks were covered in scruff. He looked exactly how he was—dangerous and just a little wild.

His friend eyed Dec up and down, then raised a brow. "How was the job?"

"The usual."

Actually, the jobs were never the same, and you were never sure what was going to happen. Providing security to archeological digs, retrieving stolen artifacts, occasionally turning some bad guys over to the authorities, doing museum security, or running remote expeditions for crazy treasure hunters...it kept things interesting.

"Anyone shoot at you?"

The female voice came from over by the computers. Morgan Kincaid sat cross-legged on top of a table. She was one of the few females to pass the rigorous BUD/S training for the Navy SEALs. But when the Navy had refused to let her serve on the teams, she'd left.

The Navy's loss was Dec's gain. Morgan was tough, mean, and hell in a firefight. She was tall, kept her dark hair short, and had a scar down the left side of her face from a knife fight.

"Not this trip," Dec answered.

"Too bad," Morgan murmured.

"All right everyone, listen up." Darcy's voice echoed in the warehouse.

They all headed over to where Darcy stood in front of her screens. Logan and Hale dropped into chairs, Morgan stayed sitting on top of the table, and Dec pressed a hip to a desk and sipped his coffee.

"Where's Cal?" he asked.

"He flew out a few days ago on another job. An anthropologist got snatched by a local tribe in Brazil."

"Hate the jungle," Logan said, his voice a growl.

"And Ronin?" Dec asked.

Ronin Cooper was another full-time Treasure Hunter Security employee. Dec kept a small full-time team and hired on trusted contractors when he needed more muscle.

"Coop's in northern Canada on an expedition."

Dec raised his brows, trying to imagine Ronin in the snow.

Hale hooted with laughter. "Shit, not too many shadows to hide in when you're in the snow."

Dec sipped his coffee again. Ronin Cooper was good at blending into the shadows. You didn't see him coming unless he wanted you to. Another former SEAL, Ronin had gotten out earlier than Dec, and had done some work for the CIA. Lean and intense, Ronin was the scary danger no one saw coming.

Dec settled back against the desk. "What's this new job?"

"An archeological dig in Egypt got attacked yesterday." Darcy pointed a small remote at her screens. A map of Egypt appeared with a red dot out in the Western Desert. "It's being run by the Rhodes University out of Massachusetts."

Dec raised a brow. Rhodes had a hell of an archeological department. They had their fingers in digs all over the world and prided themselves on some of the biggest finds in recent times. Every kid with dreams of being the next Indiana Jones wanted to study at Rhodes.

"The dig is excavating a newly-discovered tomb and surrounding necropolis," Darcy continued. "They'd recently found some artifacts." She pointed again and some images of artifacts appeared. "All gold."

Hale whistled. "Nice."

Dec's muscles tensed. He knew what was coming.

"And now the artifacts are gone." Darcy leaned back on the desk. "The head of the dig was working on the artifacts at the time and was attacked. She survived. And now, we're hired. One, to ensure no more artifacts are stolen, two to ensure the safety of the dig's workers, and three—" Darcy's blue-gray gaze met Dec's "—to recover the stolen artifacts."

Dec felt a muscle tick in his jaw. "It's Anders."

"Ah, hell." Logan tipped his head back. "This is not good."

Hale was frowning. "Who's Anders?"

"Dec has a hard-on for the guy," Morgan muttered.

Dec ignored Logan and Morgan. "Ian Anders. A former British Special Air Service soldier."

Hale's frown deepened. "Heard those SAS guys are hard-core."

"They are," Dec confirmed.

Darcy stepped forward. "Declan and Logan's SEAL team was working a joint mission with Anders' team in the Middle East."

"Caught the sadistic fucker torturing locals." Even now, the screams and moans of those people came back to Dec. A nightmare he couldn't seem to outrun. "He kept them hidden, visited them every few days. Men, women...children." Dec let out a breath. "No idea how long he'd had them there."

"You saved them?" Hale said.

"No." Dec stood and took his mug to the sink. He tipped the coffee he could no longer stomach down the drain.

"You did the right thing, Dec," Logan growled.

Silence fell. Dec was not going to talk about this.

Darcy cleared her throat. "The British Military gave Anders a slap on the wrist."

"Shit," Hale said. "So what's he got to do with stolen artifacts?"

"When he left the SAS, he got into black-market antiquities," Declan said. "We've run into him a few times on jobs."

"The guy is whacked," Logan added. "He likes to

hurt and kill. And he likes the pretty cash he gets for selling artifacts."

"And you think this is his work?" Hale looked at the screens.

Dec had learned to trust his gut. Sometimes despite the facts or evidence, despite the fact you had nothing else to go on. "Yeah, it's Anders."

"Logan, Morgan, and Hale, this is your assignment," Darcy said. "You'll head to Egypt to meet Dr. Layne Rush."

Another screen filled with a photo of a woman.

Dec blinked, feeling his belly clench, even though he'd never seen this woman before.

He wasn't even sure what warranted the gut-deep response. She was attractive, but not the most beautiful woman he'd ever seen. In the photo, she had sunglasses pushed up on her dark hair. Her hair was chocolate brown and straight as a ruler. It brushed her shoulders, except for the bangs cut bluntly just across her eyes. Her skin was so incredibly clear, not a blemish on it, and her eyes were hazel.

She had smart stamped all over her. *Hell.* Dec had a thing for smart women.

But he usually steered well clear. He wasn't made for hearts and rainbows. He'd just seen too much and done too much. His relationships generally lasted one night, and he enjoyed women who wanted the same as him— uncomplicated, no-strings sex.

"I'm going." Dec's voice echoed in the warehouse.

Darcy's beautiful face got a pinched look. "Declan—"

"No arguments, Darce. I'm going."

"You're going because of Anders," she said.

Dec glanced at the photo of Dr. Rush. "I'm going to pack."

His sister sighed and looked at Dec. "You're sure you won't change your mind."

"Nope."

Another sigh. "The jet's fueled and waiting. Logan, please keep him out of trouble."

Logan snorted. "I'm good, but I'm not that good."

Darcy shook her head. "All of you, have a good trip... and stay safe. Please."

Dec smiled, trying to break the tension. "You know me."

A resigned look crossed her face. "Yes. Unfortunately, I do. So when the trouble hits, call me."

Treasure Hunter Security

Undiscovered
Uncharted
Unexplored
Unfathomed
Untraveled
Unmapped
Unidentified
Undetected

READY FOR ANOTHER?

IN THE AFTERMATH OF AN ALIEN INVASION:

HEROES WILL RISE... WHEN THEY HAVE SOMEONE TO LIVE FOR

In the aftermath of a deadly alien invasion, a band of survivors fights on...

In a world gone to hell, Elle Milton—once the darling of the Sydney social scene—has carved a role for herself as the communications officer for the toughest commando team fighting for humanity's survival—Hell Squad. It's her chance to make a difference and make up for horrible past mistakes…despite the fact that its battle-hardened commander never wanted her on his team.

When Hell Squad is tasked with destroying a strategic alien facility, Elle knows they need her skills in the field. But first she must go head to head with Marcus Steele and convince him she won't be a liability.

Marcus Steele is a warrior through and through. He fights to protect the innocent and give the human race a chance to survive. And that includes the beautiful, gutsy Elle who twists him up inside with a single look. The last thing he wants is to take her into a warzone, but soon they are thrown together battling both the alien invaders and their overwhelming attraction. And Marcus will learn just how much he'll sacrifice to keep her safe.

Hell Squad

Marcus

Cruz

Gabe

Reed

Roth

Noah

Shaw

Holmes

Niko

Finn

Theron

Hemi

Ash

Levi

Manu
Griff
Also Available as Audiobooks!

Heart of Eon

Also Available as Audiobooks!

Galactic Gladiators

Gladiator

Warrior

Hero

Protector

Champion

Barbarian

Beast

Rogue

Guardian

Cyborg

Imperator

Also Available as Audiobooks!

Hell Squad

Marcus

Cruz

Gabe

Reed

Roth

Noah

Shaw

Holmes

Niko

Finn

Theron

Hemi

Ash

Levi

Manu

Griff

Also Available as Audiobooks!

The Anomaly Series

Time Thief

Mind Raider

Soul Stealer

Salvation

Anomaly Series Box Set

The Phoenix Adventures

Among Galactic Ruins

At Star's End

In the Devil's Nebula

On a Rogue Planet

Beneath a Trojan Moon

Beyond Galaxy's Edge

On a Cyborg Planet

Return to Dark Earth

On a Barbarian World

Lost in Barbarian Space

Through Uncharted Space

Crashed on an Ice World

Perma Series

Winter Fusion

A Galactic Holiday

Warriors of the Wind

Tempest

Storm & Seduction

Fury & Darkness

Standalone Titles

Savage Dragon

Hunter's Surrender

One Night with the Wolf

For more information visit AnnaHackettBooks.com

ABOUT THE AUTHOR

I'm a USA Today bestselling author and I'm passionate about **action romance**. I love stories that combine the thrill of falling in love with the excitement of action, danger and adventure. I'm a sucker for that moment when the team is walking in slow motion, shoulder-to-shoulder heading off into battle. I write about people overcoming unbeatable odds and achieving seemingly impossible goals. I like to believe it's possible for all of us to do the same.

My books are mixture of action, adventure and sexy romance and they're recommended for anyone who enjoys fast-paced stories where the boy wins the girl at the end (or sometimes the girl wins the boy!)

For release dates, action romance info, free books, and other fun stuff, sign up for the latest news here:

Website: www.annahackettbooks.com